A BETTER PLAN

ELISA MARIA HEBERT

In memory of Bud Steinle who servant heartedly loved his neighbors.

And to Mike, my husband, dearest friend, and my real life version of Pete from this story — I love you. Thank you for treasuring me.

For I know the thoughts that I think toward you, saith the Lord, thoughts of peace, and not of evil, to give you an expected end.
Jeremiah 29:11

I couldn't wait to get out of Vegas. I'd flown down for a three-day conference and as invigorating as I found the sun and warm weather, the city never slept. While walking down the street before eight in the morning, I had tried to call my friend, Angie, to check in and let her know all was well.

The volume of the music being piped through speakers on the strip forced me to duck into a coffee shop. It was just as loud in there, so I went back outdoors. I ended up texting her to let her know my phone wouldn't work in my hotel room and the city noise forbade having any phone conversation.

My short time in Sin City made me feel like I'd been trapped in an arcade video game. The constant pinging and other obnoxious noises emanating from gambling machines, the lights and blaring music — all things that were intended to intoxicate people with gambling fever. I found the over stimulation worse to contend with than cabin fever. Anxious to escape the manufactured chaos, I returned to my hotel, which, compared to the one where my class had been held, was rather low-key since it didn't possess a casino — the primary reason I'd chosen it. I stood in line to check out along with a number of physician assistants who were also in town for conferences, then scurried to catch a shuttle to the airport.

After going through security, I grabbed a cold drink at a kiosk and went to my gate to wait. A heavy set, boisterous man, who was clearly comfortable with drawing attention to himself, spoke loudly and to no one in particular.

I maneuvered my rolling carry-on in front of me with my back to him until my flight was called, and I merged into line to board. I displayed my boarding pass on my phone and made my way down the narrow aisle to seat 22 B — a middle seat. I never flew in the middle seat, I preferred to sit on the aisle, but they had overbooked the flight. I took a few deep breaths. Being a person who needed order and control, just thinking of sitting in the middle seat put me on the edge of panic mode. My second choice would have been the window, but those were also taken. I convinced myself I could make the almost two hour flight to Portland, although it wouldn't be pleasant. I would simply focus on the fact that I had a reserved aisle seat on my next flight.

An older, attractive, bald man sporting a full, gray, fire-man's mustache occupied seat A. As I picked up my carry-on to store it in the overhead bin, he jumped up. "May I help you with that, young lady?"

"No, thank you. It's not heavy." I smiled at him. He sat down, buckled his seatbelt and picked up his National Geographic. I stored my small shoulder bag under the seat in front of me and buckled my seatbelt. As the plane filled with passengers, I heard a loud voice and glanced up to see the man from the terminal storing his suit coat and briefcase in the overhead bin. He looked down at me and grinned. My shoulder muscles tensed to the base of my skull.

"Oh, this is my lucky day." He said as he grabbed the arm rest and dropped heavily into the aisle seat beside me. He leaned in, much too close to my face, and I could smell the liquid breakfast he'd consumed. "Looks like we're going to get to know each other up close and personal, huh, babe?" He pushed the button on the armrest between us and lifted it. "I don't know why they make these seats so small. You don't need that whole seat, honey — you don't mind sharing a little space with ol' Bucky, now do ya?"

Okay, deep breath. Two hours may be way too long. I recalled the movie, *Planes, Trains and Automobiles* and for some reason it made me laugh — briefly. *I wonder if I'd fit in the overhead bin. Or maybe I could hide in the lavatory.*

The gentleman by the window flagged a flight attendant over. "I'm sorry, miss. I'm recovering from a bout of malaria and I need to use the rest room real quick."

Oh splendid, I'm trapped between 'liquid breakfast' and 'symptoms of malaria'.

The flight attendant tapped Bucky on his shoulder. "Excuse me sir, this passenger needs to get out."

Bucky looked at her and grinned. "Sure, ma'am." As soon as he spoke she took a step back. Intoxication by conversation, I assumed. I stood and moved into the aisle after him to let the gentleman pass.

A short while later, the man returned and Bucky pushed himself up from the seat and moved into the aisle. I stood up to move out of the way so the man could get back in, but he gently put his hand on my arm and gestured for me to move over into the window seat. "Are you sure," I asked? He nodded. I squatted down to grab my handbag and slipped over before he settled into the middle seat. He put the armrest down between Bucky and himself, before giving Bucky a thumbs up.

I smiled and handed him his magazine from the seat pocket in front of me. "Thank you."

He returned my smile and reached out his hand. "Pete."

I shook his hand. "Amelia. Nice to meet you, Pete."

"Very nice to meet you, Amelia. So where are you headed on this fine day? I'm going to Portland to visit my daughter."

"Alaska."

"Alaska! I've always wanted to go there."

"Yes, it's beautiful. If you get the opportunity you should."

"So what do you and your husband do in Alaska?"

Oh, these older men are slick indeed. I'm not wearing a ring and he wants to know if I'm married. Very smooth, Pete. "I'm a nurse. You?" *Notice how I avoided your question about a husband? I'm pretty slick too, eh?*

"I guess you could say I'm a medic." He smiled and I noticed a twinkle in his glacier blue eyes. I glanced down at his magazine and noticed that he had a nice, dark tan. And his arms looked muscular. Not like a body builder — but more like a man who works for a living. I'd guess he was in his mid sixties. *He seems like a gentleman. After all, he did just set himself as a barrier between ol' Bucky and me.*

I leaned over and asked in a lowered voice, "So, Pete, do you really have malaria?"

"Once you have it, it can resurface anytime. Yes, I've had it dozens of times. But to be honest, I'm not having any symptoms this morning. I just thought you could use a friend." There was the twinkle again.

"Thank you. Yes, sometimes we all need a friend." I had to admit I was curious about this man, but I didn't want to ask too many questions and give him the wrong impression. Then again I was quite certain that I'd never see him again. "So where did you pick up malaria?"

"First time in Viet Nam. Nothing like a tropical paradise to encounter exotic diseases," he laughed.

I knew I'd guessed about right on his age if he'd been in Viet Nam. "My older brother joined the Navy when he graduated from high school. He was on an aircraft carrier but never near Viet Nam."

"Actually I got two *vacations* there," he winked.

"Pete, thank you for your service."

He nodded thoughtfully, "I came back pretty broken. And then we were greeted by protestors at the airport when we returned. Some of our fellow citizens were meaner than the enemy we fought!"

"I'm so sorry."

"Oh, no it's fine. All is forgiven and in the past."

"I was in grade school. I guess my biggest worries then were about who would be on my team playing red rover. I don't recall people protesting where I lived, but I grew up in a military town. People may have held a different perspective. I know some friends of my brother didn't return from the war. Looking back, I'm sure that must have had an impact on him. I didn't understand any of that at the time, though."

"So, are you a Christian, Amelia?"

"As a matter of fact I am! You get right to the point, don't you?" I smiled and glanced out the window.

"No time like the present. Might only get one opportunity to ask, and I would rather put myself 'out there' than to think I didn't share the most *amazing gift* with someone. I know what it's like to be on the brink of death in this life."

"That's true, I work in an ER, and often see that it only takes a second for life to change drastically — or even to end." The flight attendant brought snacks and drinks while we chatted.

Bucky, bless us all, had fallen into an alcohol induced nap, but woke himself now and then with a loud snort. At one point, the plane hit a small patch of turbulence and he awakened so startled that he threw his arms up and yelled. People turned around to look at him and Pete and I shared a giggle.

When the plane landed, Bucky awoke and wiped the drivel from his chin, then stood in the aisle and haphazardly tucked in his shirt. Pete reached up into the overhead bin and pulled my carry-on down for me.

"Thank you. The flight went by pretty quickly."

"It sure did. I enjoyed talking with you, Amelia. Be blessed. Hey, let me give you my email address — just in case you ever feel like writing or getting in touch."

He pulled a pen off his shirt lapel and wrote his email address on a corner of his magazine before tearing it off and handing it to me. I stuck it in my pocket. He turned and patted Bucky on the shoulder. "Hey, Buck, how about you let me buy you a cup of coffee?"

Once in the terminal, I found a kiosk and bought a drink on the way to my next gate. While waiting to board I contemplated my conversation with Pete. Interesting man — openly shared his faith, defended me, and didn't seem to be afraid of anything. But he was older and kind of "in your face" about Christ. I pulled the slip of paper from my pocket that he'd written his email address on and looked at it, turning it in my hand.

When my flight began boarding I dropped my empty drink cup — and the slip of paper — in a trash can, then pulled out my phone to show my boarding pass.

CHAPTER 2

At six twenty a.m., I parked in the hospital employee lot and pulled out an extension cord to plug my car into an electrical outlet. The power would come on every hour for thirty minutes, and my battery warmer would keep the car from freezing so I could drive home again. I had to pull my gloves off to get it plugged in and my fingers already ached from the cold. I put my head down against the frosty air as I sprinted to the employee door of the hospital emergency room. The ice fog smothered the building, sucking out visibility and I didn't notice the large, hazy shadow until I nearly stumbled on her. Between the ER entry and the shrubs rested a cow moose and her calf. I stopped short and changed course, the cold filled my lungs and came out in frozen puffs as I made my way to the main entrance. Once inside I crossed the foyer and swiped my ID badge on the keypad to enter the emergency room. When I pulled back my hood and unzipped my parka, a shiver ran through me, *"Brrrrr."*

Linda, a night nurse looked up from her computer charting. "Yay! I'm always so happy to see you because I know my shift is about to come to an end. It wasn't a bad night. When it's this cold the sane people stay close to home or work and the loonies stay wherever. What's the temp out there?"

"-54* — a glorious, ice foggy, dark morning in Alaska. Better start your car now and maybe it'll be warm by the time you get out there."

Linda groaned. "Sorry I asked. How long are these temps going to stick around?"

Gil, one of the emergency room technicians patted her on the shoulder. "Poor Linda, from Alabama. Your man joins the military and drags you off to Alaska, then he goes someplace warm like Iraq. What's with that?"

Linda swatted the air in his direction. "Yes, what's with that? I wanted to stay here in Alaska. I like my job and the last time he was deployed I was across the country when he came home. At least this way the kids didn't have to be moved and change schools twice. There's something to be said for continuity when you're a military family."

Dr. Fletcher came out of a patient room. "Good morning, Amelia, did you have a nice trip?" He was one of the few people I knew who used my name. Most called me Mel. He stood over six feet tall and his skin was tan from the ski vacations he fit in as often as possible.

He'd become a doctor in the Navy before civilian life, and he still maintained an athletic physique. His gentle, easy going manner made him a favorite with both the patients and the staff.

"Good morning, Doc, it's always good to have a break. I think three or four of these twelve-hour shifts in a row are enough. Our personalities start changing after that." I crossed my eyes and made a weird face.

He laughed. "That's why we docs work eight hour shifts — Dr. Jekyll and Mr. Hyde." He bugged his eyes and made a face before he sat down at his computer in the doctor's station.

In the locker room I changed into scrubs, topped them with a sweater and pulled my hair up in a loose pony tail. I looked at the clock and noted that I still had time to run to the coffee stand before I clocked in. I ordered my drink and paid the barista then I spotted Takisha, one of the night nurses, as she set down the creamer . "Hey, Takisha, isn't it a bit late for you to be drinking coffee?"

She looked up and smiled. "I have a doctor's appointment this morning after I get the kids off to school. I can't believe you guys don't close the schools when it's this cold."

"Honey, if we did that they'd have to go to school all summer and everyone would be playing hooky. Is everything okay?" The barista handed me my drink.

"Yeah, it's just a follow-up. Been cancer free for eleven months now." She lifted her drink in a salute.

"Thank God!" I tapped my cup against hers and hugged her with my other arm. "That is an answer to our prayers."

"Yes, it is and I'm so grateful you were praying for me."

At seven fifteen the medic phone rang. Being the nearest in proximity to the phone, I picked it up. "ER, This is Mel speaking."

"ER, this is medic 3, ETA fifteen minutes. Inbound with sixty-three-year old male complaining of substernal chest pain..."

"Copy that medic 3. Room two on arrival." I handed my notes from the phone call to the doctor. The staff took their positions and began setting up for the patient when the medic phone rang again.

"ER, this is medic 1. Arrived on scene to find thirty-four-year old male collapsed on gym floor with head wound. Pulseless and CPR started..."

Dr. Martinez had arrived by this time, and as he headed for the doctor's station, I handed him the notes. He would be the trauma doc for the next eight hours. Ellen, another nurse on staff, headed to the trauma room to set up while I called the departments that assist in trauma cases — lab, radiology, pharmacy, respiratory and the nursing supervisor.

Medic 3 arrived in the ambulance bay and the paramedic and EMT's brought their patient in. I helped hook the patient up to the monitors while Nicole, an RN, started an another IV. On my way back to the trauma room the medic phone rang yet again. I handed the note to Dr. Martinez and he grabbed it with one hand, taking a gulp of coffee from the mug he held in the other. "Just another day in paradise," he said. He hummed and tapped his feet as though dancing, while still in his chair.

I walked away grinning. *His coffee intake is obviously on par this morning.*

The morning passed quickly. During the winter the hospital kept a smaller number of staff than in the summer when the hospital employed additional travel nurses. The extra staff was needed to help with the influx of patients which always grew with more tourists and locals out and about enjoying summer activities such as biking, boating, running, racing and many other outdoor adventures. Since it didn't get dark, people had a lot more hours in which to play — and possibly get injured.

It was mid afternoon before I had a chance to take my thirty minute lunch break. I enjoyed the quiet of the first half of my break before my voice pager went off. "Hey, Mel, this is Grace. Sorry, but we need you back out here. There's been a three car MVA and several patients are coming."

"On my way." I tossed my lunch in the fridge hoping to

finish it later. Motor vehicle accidents in this type of weather, which created low visibility on the roads due to ice fog weren't a surprise, but with the bitter cold, chances of exposure and frostbite added an element of urgency.

Six people were brought in from the accident, three were treated and released, we set one up for surgery for a broken femur, and sent another with possible internal bleeding to the Intensive Care Unit for observation.

Security came for the sixth and final patient who was declared dead on arrival. They body bagged him and took him to the morgue. A few of us stood by reverently as they passed by. We never liked losing a patient and in the adrenaline rush of doing our best, the emotional crash of losing one was something we each had to deal with on our own terms. I always found myself praying for the family who would get the terrible news that a loved one had been lost. The phone rang and pulled me from my thoughts. "ER, this is Mel."

"Hey Mel, how ya doin'?"

"Who is this?"

"This is Leon. I've been in there a bunch of times. I guess you guys would call me a frequent flyer." He laughed at his pathetic attempt at humor.

"Leon, how did you get this number?"

"Oh, I've learned my way around the system." He laughed again.

"What do you need Leon?" I blew out a breath of exasperation.

"Well, I have a toothache. Can you fix me up?"

"I'm sorry, we don't have a dentist on call. You will need to call a dentist."

"Ah, that takes too much time and they won't see me anyway. Come on, Mel, baby."

"You need to call a dentist." I hung up and went to help

Sophie and Grace put things in order in the trauma rooms so housekeeping could come in and do their job. Both young women were in their early twenties working as CNA's while going to nursing school. We checked the oxygen tanks, hung new Ambu bags — which are used to ventilate patients — and stocked the cabinets.

Sophie let out a long sigh.

"Are you doing alright?" I asked.

She shrugged. "I met that guy — the one who died. My boyfriend snowboards and we went to a party one time and that man was there. Seemed really nice. I was kinda surprised because I guess he was a really good snowboarder for being so old."

I let the part about a man in his forties being 'so old' go. "That's the hardest thing about this job — we can only do our best. I always thought the first time I would ever have to perform CPR would be on an overweight, middle aged man."

Sophie cocked her head and said, "That's what I would imagine too. And it wasn't?"

"Nope — a sixteen-year-old-boy who had been dirt bike racing. What made it even harder was that his dad came in with him and was crying and said, 'I'm so sorry, buddy. I'm so sorry the last words I said to you were so mean.' Here I was doing CPR and my tears were falling on my patient. We couldn't save him. I felt bad for the boy, but I felt awful for his dad too. Not just the loss of his son, but the regret he'd live with. I love my job when we succeed, but when we don't, it tears out a little bit of my heart."

"How do you deal with — you know — the deaths?"

"Sophie, I'm a Christian and as a young child one of the Bible verses I memorized says, 'Your eyes saw my unformed body; all the days ordained for me were written in your book before one of them came to be. Psalm 139:16.' I believe God is not surprised when we pass from this life — we are the ones who suffer when we lose a loved one. There are things beyond my control, but one thing I can do for all my patients is pray."

"But it's still hard, isn't it? How have you managed to stay in this department so long then? Maybe I would rather be working in pediatrics ."

"I can see you working in PEDS, Sophie. I think that's a good fit for you. I worked as an IV therapy nurse for seven years and then took two years off. When I came back, the ER had an opening and I've been here for five years now. I didn't get my nursing degree in my twenties like you girls are doing. I chose to stay home and raise my two little boys. When I finished nursing school I was nearly forty-years-old. How about you, Grace? Where do you think you will want to work when you finish the nursing program?"

She smiled and lifted her head. "I want 'em before Sophie gets 'em." She giggled. "I want to work in labor and delivery." She hugged her arms to her chest. "I can't think of anything more rewarding than welcoming precious, new babies into the world and encouraging moms in the process."

The medic phone rang interrupting our chatter and I grabbed it. "This is medic 3 and we have a thirty-two-year-old male complaining of a toothache. ETA — we are approaching the ambulance bay doors."

"Okay, medic 3, we'll get them open." I hung up a little harder than I needed to. Doctor Martinez looked over at me from his computer and raised his eyebrows.

"The guy that called our number direct this morning is arriving in his royal coach with a toothache."

"How do you *really* feel about it, Mel?" Dr. Martinez laughed.

"I'm thankful I'm working trauma today and don't have to deal with this guy,' I said begrudgingly. "We have heart attacks and car wrecks and serious medical needs coming in, and this guy thinks nothing of calling an ambulance to transport him a block and a half to the ER for a toothache. And after I told him there was nothing we could do for him. Not only is he tying up services that might be a lifeline to someone truly in need, he acts like he's entitled to it. "

"Okay, I asked didn't I?"

I laughed and covered my face with my hands. "I'm sorry, my cynicism is showing."

"And I totally agree with you, young lady." He patted my shoulder as he walked by.

The next morning I made my way through the house to the kitchen. I was followed closely by my furry friends, Snowball, a white cat with one black tipped ear, and Jack Frost, my yellow lab mix. Snowball wove her way through my legs purring, while Jack obediently stood back as I poured some kibble in his bowl. I fed Snowball then made myself a brain freeze — a shot of espresso with ice, half and half, and dark chocolate. I threw in some frozen wild blueberries I picked the previous summer. I needed the shot of espresso since I found myself starting a bit slower after working four consecutive twelve-hour shifts in the ER — three of my own plus an additional one for a co-worker who was sick.

I pulled a forty pound bag of pellets from the storage closet and dumped them into the pellet stove, thankful I'd bought two tons of them in the fall. As cold as it had been I'd probably use most of them this winter. I went to my office, opened my laptop, and checked my 'to do' list, making note of an interview set up for this morning. And as every Wednesday evening, I would teach a financial advising course. Even throughout the long winter cold spell, people who committed to the class had been faithful about coming once they saw first hand that implementing the information truly could change their lives. That's one of the reasons I found leading the classes so gratifying. I enjoyed making it fun for participants. I created games with little prizes to help them grasp the concepts of each lesson, and on the last night of class I ordered a cake decorated like a credit card. Each class enjoyed the symbolism of it being cut up before they happily devoured the whole cake.

After my shower I gave the bathroom a quick wipe down. It was always so much easier to do little things like that on a regular basis than let it go and have to spend hours later to make it shine. I blow dried my hair then dressed in a navy sweater and jeans. A nice enough outfit to do an interview, as well as to teach my class. I spotted my cell phone on the desk, grabbed it and called Elizabeth, who had promised me an interview today. When she picked up, I heard her yawn. "Good morning, Elizabeth, are we still on for today?"

"Oh, shoot I overslept! I got home yesterday instead of Monday. Can I meet you at the coffee shop near the University? Maybe ten thirty?"

"That works for me. I'll buy you coffee and a bagel for allowing me to interview you."

The coffee shop wasn't too crowded since we had arranged to meet between the morning working crowd and the lunch crowd. I found a table in the back where we could talk. When Elizabeth came in I waved her over, then went to the counter to place our order.

She took her parka off, pushed her long black braid off her shoulder and smiled. "Okay, are you ready? This is my first interview for a book. I'm not sure how much help I'll be, but I'll try. I think it's so interesting that you are a nurse by day and a writer by night. Like an undercover job." She stirred her chai with a straw.

I opened my blue notebook on which I had carefully hand printed a label for the front that read 'Book Notes'. I clicked my pen. "Let's start with what made you decide to try online dating? You're a beautiful woman so it's not because you can't attract a man. And there aren't a lot of Athabaskan female bush pilots. You really are a fascinating woman, Elizabeth."

"Ha! Thank you. As a bush pilot I work with lots of men flying people in and out of the oil fields and villages. But I don't want to have a personal relationship with the guys I work with. I mean what if something went sour and you had to see each other every day, you know? And when I have to stay overnight in a bush village on a layover — well you can't really get away from each other. I'm not in town a lot and I split my time between Kodiak and Fairbanks. Add to that I'm forty-nine-years old. Is that enough reasons?"

I nodded. "I understand that there are quite a few dating sites. Did you try several or just one?"

"I tried several. Some were disastrous. I could tell you some stories! I settled on the one that had more men *in* Alaska — men with jobs, not looking for a sugar momma in Alaska to take care of them while they go fishing." We both laughed when a man at a nearby table turned and winked at her.

"Tell me how it works. What's the process?"

She took a bite of her bagel and chewed while she thought. "You answer a survey to tell about yourself and also what you are looking for in a man. They encourage you to post pictures of yourself because the profiles without any photos don't really get much attention. And I agree — who wants a blind date with someone from the internet?"

"I suppose that's true."

"Anyway, after you do all this, you can look at profiles of the guys and if you're interested in corresponding you can let them know and vice versa."

"Did you find many men that you wanted to contact?"

"Yes, amazingly, well — not many but a handful. It was

tough with my schedule, but there was a guy in Fairbanks and also one near Kodiak that seemed like possibilities. And since there are far more men than women in Alaska, they have less choice. You know what they say…."

"Yes, about the men in Alaska 'The odds are good but the goods are odd.'" We both laughed at the old cliche. A young man who looked to be in his early twenties with tangled long red hair had just walked by our table and threw his napkin in a trash can. He gave us snarly look and tossed his hair with an exaggerated shake of his head. We both cracked up laughing. When he went out the door I said, "Point taken."

"Anyway, I arranged to meet the guy from Fairbanks when I was going to be in town and we met at Gold Diggers restaurant for prime rib. He came across as a gentleman and we talked until eleven thirty that night. We had to give up our table and sit in the bar because the place is always so busy, but it didn't matter. We agreed to meet again that weekend."

"So are you still seeing him?" I leaned forward so she could feel free to speak softly.

"No, we dated — if you can call it that with me being out of town most of the time — for several months. But it ended up he really wanted someone he could spend more time with. He said it was hard to be in a relationship with me because he was more lonely knowing that I wasn't available than he was before he knew me." A shadow crossed her face.

"Wow, I'm sorry."

"It's okay, really. A few months later I activated my profile again and met Bill. He's the one who is down by Kodiak. He's a commercial fisherman. We have been steady when I'm in Kodiak, and when I'm in Fairbanks for at least a week he tries to come up to visit too since it's not fishing season. It's not amazing, but it's nice."

She looked out the window and waved at a lady getting

into a car. "We get along okay, it's better than always being lonely. Mel, instead of asking all the people you know about their experiences on the match sites, why don't you just get first hand knowledge?"

I put my chin on my hand and looked at her questioningly. Tension snaked it's way up through my abdomen and into my neck.

She sipped the last of her chai. "Seriously, the only way to understand the whole online thing is to just try it. Fill out a profile and then you can access the site and see how it all works and you can write from your own experience. I mean I love you and enjoy having chai and bagels, but just try it yourself."

"I don't date."

She shrugged her shoulders. "Then don't, but you never know."

I arrived home after ten o'clock that night, shoulders tight from my drive through the thick ice fog after financial advising class. I turned on some soothing worship music, put on fleece pajamas, wrapped up in a quilt, and dropped onto the sofa — hardly landing before Jack Frost and Snowball snuggled next to my feet and in my lap. I opened a book and realized I'd read the same paragraph several times as Elizabeth's words, *not amazing*, ran though my head. What would be amazing?

Elizabeth had talked to me before about feeling like something was missing in her life. I knew that if we deposit all our hope in a person thinking they will pay out happiness, we will end up emotionally bankrupt. I knew that well. A person can't fill a God sized void. And it isn't fair to expect them to either.

CHAPTER 3

aby It's Cold Outside, the ringtone on my phone, beckoned me. I answered without looking at the caller ID. "Hello?"

"Hey stranger, how's life in the arctic?"

Even though it was after nine in the morning and still dark outside, I felt my spirit lighten at the sound of my dear friends' voice. "Angie, it's so good to hear from you. How are you and how is the job in Seattle going?"

"The job is fine. The weather is wet. Driving in this traffic is nuts. I'm missing you. So distract me and tell me what exciting things are you doing today?"

I walked into the living room and cuddled up in the chair next to the pellet stove. "I'm not sure you could call it exciting, but I've been sitting in front of my computer doing research until I'm cross-eyed."

"Is this for the book you're working on? I can't wait to read it. I better get the first copy."

"No, this is research for starting my new life. I have a notebook full of stats. Lists of my potential cities with pros and cons. Everything from crime rates to quality of life and real estate markets. I've looked into building contractors and neighborhoods in my top contending cities. I know I want to be somewhere with seasons, but milder winters are a must. And it can't be too hot or humid. And I'd prefer somewhere near a college or university so I can take classes to expand my horizons; a place that offers culture so I can attend concerts and community events. And of course I want to find a church where I can serve and fellowship."

Angie laughed. "Oh you crack me up. You and your constant lists to keep life all orderly. And you do such a good job. I need you to come visit and organize my apartment for me. It's been a year and I still have unpacked boxes. What color is the 'moving' notebook?"

"Red, for important, and you know how I feel about boxes that haven't been opened in a year. You don't need what's inside."

"You've been in Alaska all your life. How will you leave? I mean you're thinking of all the details, but that place is in your DNA. You'll miss it terribly. And what about all your friends?"

I gazed out my window and caught the first glimpse of light sneak up over the horizon. I could see Denali Mountain from my perch by the fire. "I do feel torn about leaving, but I'm tired of rushing from car to building, and building to car. And last week Jack Frost got frostbit on his paws. I felt so awful. I promised him we would move somewhere that he could go outside any time of the year and take nice walks. Even two of the docs have gotten frostbitten this winter already and it's not even Thanksgiving! And I can make new friends. You know the saying, 'make new friends but keep the old, the new are silver and the old are gold.'"

"I understand, Mel. I sure don't miss winter up there. Not that I *love* Seattle traffic, but I have a good job, a cute apartment, and for now it works for me. I know the last few years have been really difficult for you since Jeff was killed."

My light mood dissipated as quickly as daylight on a winter day in Alaska. "Angie, I need to go. It was so good to hear your voice. I'll talk to you later. Love you." Snowball had crawled up in my lap and I absentmindedly stroked her head.

I could hear the regret in Angie's voice. "Mel, I'm sorry."

"Don't worry about it, Ang. I have gone through the healing and forgiveness process, but I see no reason to linger in that season. Life goes on and I have to as well. They say don't make any drastic changes for a year after a divorce or death and I didn't. In fact I'm several years beyond that now and I'm tired of the winters and I'm tired of avoiding people who knew Jeff and heard bits of what had been going on. It's like you're walking down the street and someone zips by driving through a mud puddle and splashes you. You weren't in the puddle, but you wear it just the same."

"Oh Mel, I know you've gone through healing, I can hear hope in your voice and plans. I'm a ditz. You've created a new life. And I'm so proud of you. I'm thankful to be your friend. And I love you."

We said goodbye and I clicked my phone off, stood up and set Snowball on the chair to stay cuddled by the fire. Jack was at my feet loyally waiting to see which way I stepped so he could follow.

"Hey, Jack, how about we make some cookies?"

He wagged his tail and barked.

"Okay, we'll make some pumpkin, peanut butter treats for you because you are such a good boy, and I'll make chocolate chip cookies to take to work. They all love to be fed. And I feed them to love on them." I patted his head, washed my hands and pulled out ingredients. We hung out in the kitchen for the next few hours, me chatting and him agreeing in adoration. Gotta love a guy like Jack.

~

It was quiet Sunday morning in the ER; Nicole and I did the medicine inventory and Ellen took the time to go over some procedures with Sophie and Grace. She was thorough, patient and had many years of experience. I admired so many things about her.

When I work on Sundays, I try to go to church on Saturday night but last night I didn't feel like driving to town in the cold. I wish I had forced myself to make the drive because now I felt like I had skipped a main meal. I glanced at the clock — nine thirty a.m. and we only had a couple of patients with minor issues. Nicole was the charge nurse today so I caught her. "Nicole think I could take my lunch break now?"

"But it's so early, you'll be wiped out by six thirty tonight."

"I'll be fine. There's a church a few blocks from here and I'd like to go. I'll keep my pager on just in case."

"Oh, sure Mel. Go ahead and go. We won't page you unless we absolutely have to."

I hugged her. "Thanks, you're the best."

When I arrived and slipped into a back seat, the worship team was still singing. A young couple beside me noticed my scrubs and pager and the young man leaned over towards me. "Hospital?"

I nodded and smiled.

"Thank you for being willing to serve even on a Sunday."

My heart warmed. I could tell he was military and here he was thanking me. I turned my focus to why I had come and I was intentional about worship. I sang along during the last song and listened to the message with an open heart. At the end of the service I slipped out before the pastor finished praying so I could get out of the parking lot quickly and back to work.

Katy from radiology brought a patient back and leaned over the counter. "How's it going, guys?"

Nicole said, "Great. My daughter just got a job with the railroad and my son made the cross country ski team."

"That is great, Nicole, your kids are so sweet. I'm glad they're doing well." I turned to Katy. "How about you? Anything new?"

"I'm dating a guy, kinda. I met him at the bar last weekend and he took me back to his place."

My heart ached for Katy. She was young and vibrant and seemed to go through boyfriends like boxes of chocolates. She consistently met them all in local bars, and they were long gone within a couple of months. Each guy she dated left her a little more broken hearted. I cared about her and wanted to tell her to guard her heart, but how could I convey that to her?

She looked at me. "What about you, Mel? You know I don't even know, are you married? I've heard you talk about your sons, but never about a husband."

"No, I'm not."

She stood up and did a little cheerleader move. "Oh wow, that is so cool. My dad would adore you. Let me hook you guys up. What's your phone number? I know he'll call right away. Oh, this is so exciting!"

I coughed. "That's really sweet, Katy, but I don't date."

"Seriously, you gotta meet my dad. He'll flip over you!"

"Katy, *I don't* date."

"Well, did you have a bad divorce or what?"

"Nicole I'm going to check the oxygen tanks. See ya later, Katy." I could feel sweat on the back of my neck as I escaped to the equipment room. One reason I came to the ER was that only a couple of people knew me from when I worked in IV therapy. I left the hospital when Jeff was killed. I was so ashamed and humiliated I couldn't go to work wondering how much my co-workers knew. I managed to keep my private life private since taking this job. Not that people didn't ask questions, but I had learned to gracefully dodge them. Katy had no boundaries or filter and usually when she came in and got chatty it was with the younger staff. Today totally caught me off guard.

Thanksgiving morning I packed a container of sugar cookies I'd made the day before. Maple leaves, even though we didn't have maple trees in Alaska, they were associated with Thanksgiving in the cookie cutter department. There were also cookies shaped like turkeys, and pumpkins, which I had frosted accordingly. I'd also made chicken enchiladas — not a turkey dinner, but something I could transport easily to share with my coworkers for our holiday meal at work. I knew most of them would have the meal after work or tomorrow, but I wouldn't since I lived alone.

When I arrived at work, Josh, 28, and Christy, 31, both nurses, met me coming in the door and volunteered to take my offering to the break room. "How do you know I brought anything," I said teasingly.

Josh grinned, "We can count on you. You always bring treats. You're like a mom to us."

I pulled out the container of cookies from the box I was holding and handed it to him. "Yes, and you guys are like my kids. Put the metal pan in the fridge would you? It's for lunch." I felt warm inside even though I shivered when I took off my coat and scarf to change into my scrubs. I loved the *kids* I worked with. I cared about them. Sometimes I wanted to put them in time out and other times I wanted to hug them.

The day was fairly quiet. No accidents or heart attacks. There was an elderly man with influenza who we admitted for hydration, and a two year old with a peanut candy up her nose, the standard stuff.

The staff enjoyed the enchiladas — no one really took a full lunch break. They just heated up a plate of food when they got hungry. In the afternoon during an exceptional lull, we cleaned and organized the cabinets in the exam rooms. I made labels so things would get put back and restocked neatly — I hoped — and then we sat down and shared cookies while waiting for the next patient.

Between bites of cookie I asked, "So who's going shopping tomorrow morning?"

Christy said, "I am; I'm going to get my Christmas shopping done in one day then I can party till Christmas!"

"I'm not going near the stores, thank you very much," Josh said.

Dr. Fletcher asked, "What are your plans, Amelia?"

"Hmm, I have always loved Christmas and this is the first one since I was a teenager that I won't have any family around. I thought about getting depressed but it wasn't on my list, so I decided to do some things I haven't done before instead."

He nodded. "Such as?"

"This weekend I have things to do at home and then I'm going to enjoy the season."

Christy lit up. "Parties?"

"No, nothing you would consider a party. I've never been to the Nutcracker Ballet and the local Ballet Society performs it every year so I'm going to attend it this year. And there's a concert at the University as well. I also signed up to work Christmas Day so someone with family around can be with them, and I won't be home wishing my family was around."

"I'm working too," Josh put in. "So you'll be bringing treats again, right, *mom*?" He said.

I laughed, "Of course. Would I make my kids go without treats on Christmas? Heaven forbid!"

There were paper clips on the counter by the phone. I grabbed them to put them in the container and found someone had hooked them all together in a chain. "Oh my word, someone must have been terribly bored and uncreative."

Christy leaned her rolling chair back and laughed. "Miss neat freak, will that send you into a panic attack?"

"No, because I'm granting you the honor of separating them." I held them out and she took them.

One of the medics, Dan, walked in the back door, came up to the counter and leaned his elbows on it. "Who's having a panic attack? Help is here," He wiggled his eyebrows and grinned.

I said, "No one is having a panic attack. What are you doing here?"

He stood up. I guessed he was about six feet four inches, with a short military style haircut, blue eyes, broad shoulders and deep voice that soothed like a cat purr. "We got called out to a well being check and had to pass by here, so just I stopped in to see how everyone's doing on this fine Thanksgiving Day."

Josh looked Dan up and down and said, "Man, you must work out all the time. Do you use supplements?"

Dan looked over at him. "Do you go to the gym? I can meet up with you and walk you through my routine. We'll get you in great shape in no time."

"Awesome, dude, thanks," Josh said.

Dr. Fletcher smiled. "Oh *dude* can I come too?"

Dan laughed. "Sure old man, maybe we can do something with that body of yours."

I watched Dan leave and said, "I have such a crush on him."

Christy was still pulling apart paper clips and stopped to

look over at me. "What? You don't even date. And I think he's even married!"

I laughed. "Christy, honey, you don't have to be in the house buying market to appreciate the real estate."

She looked puzzled and Dr. Fletcher busted out laughing. "Good one, Amelia, good one."

At the end of the day I drove home thanking God for my many blessings. A job to support myself that also allowed me to care for others. A warm house to return to, a reliable car to get me there, Jack Frost and Snowball to welcome me home, co-workers I loved, and a hope for the future. I also thanked Him for the breathless beauty of Alaska which daily reminded me of the greatness and vastness of God's love and creativity.

An older song by Third Day, *Show Me Your Glory*, came on the radio and I sang along making it a prayer when suddenly the sky burst with the Northern Lights. Green, yellow, red and purple waves of color lit up the sky, swirling and dancing as if directed by the baton of a mighty conductor. I felt so overwhelmed by the beauty that I had to pull over to the side of the road to enjoy it. I sat there in the dark, awestruck. Tears welled in my eyes.

Lord, thank you for showing me a hint of your Glory. You painted the skies with your spectacular brush strokes — your love spills over. Oh, to be able to share this moment with someone else. It's too special for me alone.

Child, you are never alone. I will be with you always.

I'd sat in my idling car watching the display for about fifteen minutes when a pickup truck pulled beside me and the passenger window rolled down. A young man in a fur hat with long hair sticking out from under it, and a wanna-be beard on his face leaned his head out. I lowered my window.

"Are you okay?" He asked.

"Oh, yes, I'm fine. Thank you for stopping." I gave him a

thumbs up and smiled. He nodded, rolled the window up and they drove on. I noticed the marijuana sticker on the tailgate. I laughed at the reminder that God can use anyone for his purposes. *Lord, thank you for watching over me.* I pulled back onto the road and drove home — with my heart rather than my belly — filled with thanksgiving.

Saturday morning I pulled up my Christmas playlists and chose classical strings, then pulled out the decorations. When my sons, Leighton and Tyson were growing up, our tradition was to put the tree up and decorate the house the weekend after Thanksgiving. I decided since I was celebrating Christmas that I would carry-on the tradition.

I assembled the artificial tree and made sure all the lights were in working order.

When my boys were toddlers, I made cloth ornaments so that when they crawled under the tree and reached for the decorations they could not be hurt. When they got to an age of no longer being enticed by the dangling temptations, we had kittens or puppies so I had kept the non breakables. I also had mini chimes that hung on the lowest branches so that I always knew if the tree was being disturbed. Jack Frost sniffed the ornaments no doubt smelling all the Christmases of the past while Snowball batted at the chimes.

"You are not going to do that all night, Miss Snowball," I scolded the cat. Her tail went up in the air as did her nose and she hopped up in the window sill to watch chickadees at the bird feeder — and to ignore me, no doubt.

Once the tree was finished, I hung a large wreath on the stone fireplace and stockings for Jack and Snowball. The more I decorated, the more my spirit lifted and instead of thinking about not having family around this year, I remembered many happy times we had as they grew up and the last few years when Leighton and his wife and three children lived next door. The kids had worn a path between our houses coming to beg for cookies and stories when they were small children, and later years just to hang out, share popcorn and a movie or play games. The kids were in fifth and sixth grade when they moved.

Leighton and his wife Jeannie tried to get me to move with them to Wyoming, but I needed to live my life, not be a fifth wheel in theirs. And if I had moved then, it would have been mainly for the grandkids and they were growing pretty independent. I had also wondered, what would I do with myself in Wyoming?

My stomach rumbled and I glanced at the clock to see that it was after two o'clock in the afternoon. I went to the kitchen and pulled some veggies out of the fridge, cut up a chicken breast and made myself a stir fry. I added cashews, a bit of fish sauce, and hot peppers, then sat down at the table. I got back up and got a cloth napkin, and a placemat, then lit the candle on the table sat back down. *Thank you, God, for your provision. And thank you for this Christmas season.*

～

Tuesday, my third consecutive day in the ER, I ended up working fourteen hours straight, because I covered for Linda who had to pick up her babysitter whose car wouldn't start. By the time I got home and took care of Jack and Snowball, got my shower, and threw in a load of wash, I was too tired to sleep. I got on my laptop and did a search for dating sites. I hadn't touched my notes or done anything with my writing in over two weeks.

There were so many sites touting everything from marriage to quick 'hook ups'. I wasn't interested in 'hook ups' and I only needed to understand the process and collect enough data to make my story believable. After all, it was going to be a clean romantic fiction. Overwhelmed, I closed the laptop turned on some music and stretched out on the sofa. I woke with my arms and legs cold — my stomach was warm because Snowball slept curled up on me. I lifted her off, brushed my teeth and went to bed just after three in the morning.

Saturday I called my friend, Pam, who was a social worker. "Pam, good morning! I'll cook you brunch if you'll help me work on my writing project."

"I'd be happy to help, but I'm not sure what I can do."

"Just show up around ten thirty and we'll talk."

"Okay, I'll be there. Can I bring anything?"

"No, just yourself, and your thinking cap. See you in a while." I turned on a classical strings Christmas playlist and went to the kitchen where I pulled out bacon, spinach, eggs and cheese to make a crustless quiche. I cooked the bacon to crisp, then assembled the remaining ingredients and placed the quiche in the oven. I cut up apples, rinsed grapes and arranged them both in a crystal dish and set them in the center of the table. By the time Pam arrived, the table was set with china, silver, brocade napkins, and the coffee I'd made in the French press.

Pam shivered as she closed the door and came into the living room. She handed me her coat and moved toward the pellet stove as I hung her coat up on the rack by the door. She knelt down to greet Jack Frost and give Snowflake a pet. "I love your tree and decorations. It looks so festive in here. And it smells divine."

"Coffee?"

She followed me into the dining room. "Wow, Mel. I feel so special. Look at this table!"

"You are special. Go ahead and sit down." I poured her coffee and set the silver creamer pitcher in front of her before I sat across from her. "Mind if I say grace?"

She made a sweeping gesture with her hand. "Not at all, I know you're a praying woman."

After I said grace, we ate and chatted about the weather, work and the latest happenings in our lives for a bit.

"Okay, now that you've plied me with a gourmet meal and good coffee, what can I do?"

"You know I'm trying to write another book. The last one took me three years because it was such a difficult subject, so this time I want to write something lighthearted. I decided to write a romance."

She wrapped her hands around her second cup of coffee. "Hmm, interesting. Is so that you can live vicariously? I mean since you don't date?"

"Not at all! When writing one can create the perfect world, perfect relationship, and the perfect messes because you actually have control. Let's go sit in the living room by the fire." I got up and led the way.

"So go ahead. Pick my brain." She pulled her feet under her and I slid the quilt from the back of the sofa towards her. She set her coffee down and wrapped the quilt around herself. Snowball watched with interest and as soon as Pam was settled, Snowball jumped in her lap and snuggled in. "I love cats. They are so soothing."

"Yes, especially when you have a quilt between you and their claws so you can't feel the kneading." I imitated kneading claws in the air. "Okay, I have done a few interviews with people who met spouses or boyfriends online. One friend told me that I should set up a profile on one of the sites so that I can understand how it works. The thing is, I did a search and there are so many sites for about everything you can imagine. And maybe some you can't." I raised one eyebrow.

Pam laughed. "So will you actually date someone then?"

"No, and I don't know which site to use."

"Well, you could set up a profile on a few." She leaned forward. "In fact you could make up a different profile for each site. Be several different people." Her eyes grew large and she rubbed her hands together. " Oh, you could have fun with this, Mel."

"But Pam, that's my dilemma — I don't want to lead people on. I don't want to lie either. Maybe this whole thing is a bad idea."

"What's your story line?"

"My protagonist wants to find love but is insecure about her looks so she avoids meeting anyone. She decides to try online dating, but agonizes over how to post pictures when she is self conscious about — whatever — her nose or cheekbones or thighs or something. So she decides to get plastic surgery. The surgeon asks her why she wants to have surgery and she confides in him about her insecurity. Meanwhile he finds her sense of humor delightfully refreshing and while she's trying to 'fix' something to impress people she doesn't know, he's falling for her."

"It sounds like it could be a romantic comedy. You *could* have a lot of fun with this. Hmm. Why don't you just set up a real profile then?"

"Why would I do that?" Jack nudged my hand with his nose and I scratched his ear.

"You're struggling with pretending to be someone you aren't, so just be yourself."

"But what about pictures? I wouldn't want anyone here to see my profile and think I'm looking to date. Oh, I know! I could set up a real profile but post it in another state where I don't know anyone. What do you think?"

"That's perfect! You could even post a picture then because it would be no threat — I mean they aren't going to run into you at the grocery store. But what will you do when men contact you?"

"I'm sure that won't be a problem. I'm in my fifties."

Pam rolled her eyes.

'You didn't just roll your eyes at me. I guess you're right though. I should be prepared in the off chance some guy will write, huh? I don't want to be mean so maybe I could answer with a note. How about, 'thank you for your interest but I'm currently communicating with someone.' Would that be okay?"

"Absolutely, then you aren't crushing anyone." She rubbed her hands together. "Well, now that we have solved all that, I guess I should go home and decorate. Your house is so festive it inspires me."

I hugged Pam at the door. "Thank you for your input and friendship."

"Anytime. I'm thankful for your friendship, Mel. Are you still seriously thinking about moving?"

I nodded.

"Because if you do, you'll be missed. I hope you know that."

I watched her car disappear down the driveway, the exhaust creating its own pattern of ice fog in the cold. The sun which barely rises above the horizon this time of year, glistened in the trees that Alaska had beautifully frosted with her icy fingers.

CHAPTER 4

*a*fter spending over an hour checking out sites, I had narrowed it down to two. I found that one of them had an incredibly long process of telling everything about yourself and they promised a good match. Since I was looking for story fodder, not a match, I chose the less complicated one.

The questionnaire began simply enough once I chose a user name — Crystal — no one had to know I chose it because this time of year I felt like an ice crystal.

HEIGHT: 5'7" WEIGHT: 128 lbs HAIR: blond EYES: blue

CHURCH: interdenominational ENERGY LEVEL: high

FIELD OF WORK: medical RELATIONSHIP STATUS: widowed

FAVORITE ACTIVITIES: mountain biking, hiking, cooking, time with friends and family.

It was a lot like filling out a job application, except this didn't ask what employers sometimes asked — 'what is your greatest strength?' That question perplexed me until I had worked in the ER for a while, then I had an answer — I do well with people on the worse day of their life.

I went to the kitchen, poured some almonds in a bowl and grabbed a bottle of water. Twenty minutes passed before I went back into my office. It took another couple of hours to process my thoughts on dozens of sticky notes until I had my work surface covered with colorful squares. The next part I found particularly exhausting. I guess because if I was going to answer the questions for real, I had to do some thinking and soul searching.

If I wasn't just doing this for research, but honestly looking for companionship, how would I answer?

INTRODUCTION: A friend pointed out that my dog is just like me so maybe I need to describe him and you'll know more about me so here goes. Faithful, playful, lives life with exuberance, loves people, loves together time but likes to be alone sometimes too. Appreciates good food, long nature walks and sitting by the fire. Loves affection and frequently wags tail — no wait, that part doesn't apply to me.

Maybe who I'm looking for would be easier to describe in his terms as well;

Leader, faithful, spends time doing things together, steady, dependable, good conversation, laughter, looks out for me.

I'm not a high maintenance lady. (Well, except Honey-crisp apples. They are the Lamborghini of the apple kingdom and I'm totally hooked on them.) Places I've called home range from a remote cabin with neither electricity or running water, to a modern house with all the amenities. Have accomplished things both out of necessity and a sense of adventure. I appreciate God's handiwork. I love CHRIST-MAS! The Hope, the Spirit, the music, the sappy movies, the lights, cooking, fellowship. (not the malls so much.)

I find intelligence attractive, as well a man who can take charge, not a bully. A man who puts wings on his dreams to make them happen.

You don't need to tell me if you look young for your age or are handsome. If you have a photo, I can figure it out for myself. Those are not qualities, they are traits. Traits that you have little or no control over, (unless you picked your parents).

On a deeper level, I'm acutely aware of how fragile and precious life is and witness with much frequency how a split second decision by one person can impact many lives.

ESSAY QUESTIONS:

Q: What I'd like to do on a first date...

A: Something casual or working on a project together. Just getting to know each other. Throw me a stick?

Q: My past relationships have taught me...

A: Life is not fair. God is just and faithful to complete what he starts. He started me and He will complete me.

Everyone should have their own tube of toothpaste so they can squeeze it however they want.

Q: To me, being a Christian means...

A: Knowing I'm a child of God and He disciplines those He loves for their good. I am loved unconditionally. I have a responsibility to use the gifts He has given me for His Glory. Listening for Him — which melts my heart when He speaks to me through His Word. Being a voice for the voiceless, I abhor the mistreatment of children and animals.

Q: What is your definition of love?

A: The best definition of love I've heard was by a man named Ed Cole. I don't remember the exact words but the gist of it was;

'The desire of love is to give.

The desire of lust is to get.'

Q: What does being a Spiritual Leader mean to you?

A: One who hears the voice of the Shepherd and responds

and looks out for the 'young' or vulnerable under his/her care. One who speaks truth in love.

Q: What's the last thing that made you laugh?

A: My dog. He is SO adorable and makes me laugh every day at his antics.

I didn't hit 'submit' on my profile. I wanted to let it settle before I made the no-turning-back decision to put myself out there. Even though I listed my location as Arizona, I had a niggling fear. Fear of what? I couldn't answer that.

By the time I closed my laptop I had brain strain, the sun had long since set and my stomach rumbled. I went to the fridge, got a serving of quiche, popped it in the microwave, then topped it with salsa. While I ate, Jack whined and Snowball wove around my ankles to let me know they needed attention. I rinsed my dishes and went to the living room and sat on the floor to scratch chins and rub bellies.

More than a week passed since I posted my profile, and I'd finished wrapping and packing gifts for Leighton's family and had purchased a gift certificate for Tyson, and had them all ready to mail. I'd filled spaces in Leighton's box with candy kisses for the kids and stuck the extra kisses in my purse. I drove to town and stood in line at the post office. An elderly man stood behind me and grumbled. "Christmas. Bah. Humbug. Can't even go to the post office without standing in lines like cattle to the slaughter. I've had enough of all of it. They oughta outlaw the whole darn thing."

I turned around to see who he was talking to and found everyone in line seemed to be avoiding looking at him. A gentleman behind him glanced over at me and shrugged. I smiled then touched the elderly man on the arm. "Would you like to go ahead of me? I have a couple of packages to mail and they seem to be short a person at the window today."

He tapped his toe on the floor. "Nah, you just go on ahead, I don't have anywhere to go anyway."

"Are you sure? Because I don't mind. I knew there would be a line this time of year." I reached into my purse and pulled out the kisses and opened my palm to the man. "It's the season of love, isn't it? How about a candy kiss?"

He looked at my offering, then at my face. "You know how to charm an old man, don't you?" A small smile crept over his face like a stream on parched, cracked ground. He took three candies. But to my surprise he offered one to the gentleman behind him, then the others to two children standing nearby. He looked back to me. "Thank you, lady."

"You're welcome. Merry Christmas!" I pulled the rest of the candy out and placed it in his hand. "I think you'll find purpose for the rest of these."

After I left the post office I drove to *The Book and Bean*, a popular book store and coffee shop. I wanted to get Francine River's latest book for Angie for Christmas. I located the book, paid for it, then went to the coffee counter to order a drink. A girl with short blue hair took my order, handed it to the barista and came back to take the next order.

Behind me a familiar male voice said, "I'll have a tall americano and I'm paying for her order as well."

I turned. "Dr. Fletcher, I never see you out and about."

"We aren't at work, Mel. You know my name is Mitch. Are you in a rush or do you have time to sit down with your drink?"

I hoped my surprise didn't show. "I'm not in a rush. My stop here completes my list for today." We moved over to wait on our drinks and then he put his hand on the small of my back and guided me to table off to the side. "Thank you for the drink." I hung my coat on the back of my chair.

He pulled a chair near to mine and sat down. "You're welcome. I saw you paying for your book and wanted to catch you and ask if you wanted a coffee but you beat me to the counter. I was afraid you were leaving. You look different with clothes on — I mean without scrubs on." He looked frustrated.

I tried not to laugh because I understood what he meant. I'd been on vacation once and saw a nurse who worked in the department next to mine, sitting on the beach. It took me over an hour to realize where I knew her from. She was nearly unrecognizable without her scrubs and a cap covering her brown hair — and I'd realized I'd always pictured her as blonde. I glanced around the room then back to him."So, have you been out Christmas shopping? You have two daughters, right?"

"Actually I'm out *not* shopping but I'm trying, and yes, two daughters. My oldest is married and lives in California. My younger daughter, Violet is finishing up at the University here."

"I've seen her come in the ER before to borrow your car, I think. She plays basketball doesn't she?"

"Yes, she does borrow my car on occasion and she is quite good at basketball."

"She got her height from you. What are her plans when she finishes school?"

He turned his napkin in circles on the table. "Her mom is in Colorado and I think she wants to go live there a while. When her mom moved and filed for divorce, Violet wanted to stay with me, but I think she knows I'll be okay and she can go take on the world. She's finishing a business degree.

"I'm sorry, Dr. — er — Mitch. I try not to be nosey about my coworkers. I guess I didn't know you were divorced."

"Really?" He leaned forward with his arms on the table. "That's refreshing, I guess that's how you stay so positive all the time. Stay out of other people's dirt. How about you, Mel? Did I hear you that you're a widow?"

"I don't know what you heard. I certainly didn't offer anything about my personal life at work." As soon as the words were out of my mouth I realized how defensive I sounded.

He sat up. "I'm sorry. Did I cross into forbidden territory?"

Embarrassed, I stirred my drink with a straw while I felt the blood flow to my face. "I'm sorry. You and I have worked together for five years and have shared so much as part of the team. You've always been great to work with. It's nothing personal — it's just that I pretty much avoid questions that involve relationships. I'm not comfortable talking about my personal life or mixing it into my professional life. Yes, I was widowed. My younger son, Tyson left when his dad died and has been searching the world to find himself. My older son and his family moved away last March when he took a job in Wyoming."

He reached over and put his hand over mine, leaned close and spoke softly. "I was being nosey. Please forgive me. I would never want to make you uncomfortable."

I smiled and nodded. "All is well, Mitch." We sat there making small talk for a while and observed shoppers. I looked up and saw one of the phlebotomists standing right outside the coffee area, texting like crazy with both thumbs. I wondered how they did that. She looked up with a big grin on her face when her eyes met mine. I turned back to Mitch. "This was a pleasant surprise, running into you. Thank you again for the coffee."

"My pleasure. You're always bringing treats to everyone else at work, it's the least I can do. So this was it on your list, huh? You going home now?" He took my empty cup and napkin along with his and stood to throw them in the trash.

"Yes, I need to do get some things done. It's Christmas season, you know. You have shopping to do and I have goodies to bake." I gave him a sideways hug, grabbed my shopping bag and left to get in my cold car. I realized we had chatted for over an hour.

On the drive home I replayed our encounter. A few months ago we had lost a young patient and I'd been distraught. We were all trying to process through it and while I stood at the nurses station unable to control my tears, Mitch had come up and put his arm around my shoulders to comfort me.

I thought nothing of it at the time, as sometimes we all needed each other to deal with the trauma that we saw on a regular basis. But today, not work related, the touch of his hand on the small of my back and when he touched my hand — I had to admit it was nice.

At home I mixed up some cookie dough and set it in the fridge to chill, then went to my office and pulled up the profile I had filled out. I reread it then clicked 'submit'. I added a picture that Nicole had taken of me before a reception at the hospital, then exhaled and closed the laptop. I didn't realize I'd been holding my breath.

Later I hummed along with the Christmas music while Jack Frost followed me around the kitchen hoping I'd drop some cookie dough. When the last cookies were baked and the kitchen cleaned up, I curled up on the sofa with Snowball and watched a Christmas movie. There were three generations of couples in the movie. The grandmother had been widowed and remarried and at the end, her second husband had a heart attack and died. She was distraught and her son told her, 'Mom you'll be okay. You were married to dad for forty-three years and you were okay.'

She replied, 'Yes, I had forty-three years with him and this time I only had six and it wasn't enough.' Tears streamed from my eyes and down my cheeks. Jack Frost sat up and looked concerned.

"It's okay, boy. I don't know where the tears came from." I slid to the floor, held him close and let the tears run their course.

The ice fog was always thickest along the river where the town had been established during the gold rush days. I parked my car and rushed to the ER entrance. I sang a Christmas song while I changed into my scrubs and pulled my hair up in a loose bun, and was still singing on my way to the coffee stand.

"Your usual?" the barista asked.

"Yes, thank you. How has your week been, Miss Debbie?"

Her face lit up. *"Amazing!"* She held out her left hand where a diamond sparkled on her ring finger.

"You're engaged? Congratulations, Debbie. Do you have a date set?"

"We're talking about August — before school starts. I have to go in the fall to finish up the last of my classes and that would give us time to take a honeymoon." Her smile radiated through her eyes.

"That's wonderful! I'm truly happy for you." She came around the counter to hand me my drink and I hugged her.

I clocked in and went into the ER to start my workday. I set my covered drink down by the computer and logged on. Linda came over and dropped into the chair beside me.

"Mel? Anything interesting happening in your life lately?" She grinned.

"No, nothing unusual. I have everything on my lists marked off, gifts purchased and mailed, cards mailed, cookies baked. I'm on track for Christmas. Oh, I went to the concert at the University Friday night and it was wonderful. The finale had people on their feet and you could feel the Christmas Spirit in the air."

"Really? That's great! And nothing else to report?"

"Um, no. My life is pretty orderly, Linda. I try to keep it that way."

She laughed and touched my shoulder. "Yes, you do. You're the most orderly person I know. I'm off to get a couple hours of sleep then I'm taking the kids to North Pole to see Santa. Have a super day, Mel."

"You too. Tell Santa hi for me. And make sure the kids get to pet the reindeer. I haven't been out there since I took my grandkids a couple years ago. They complained they were too old but they didn't mind getting the special North Pole hot chocolate with extra whipped cream and looking at ornaments and gifts." I smiled at the memory, but inside a little pang shot through me knowing it would be my first Christmas without any family around. I sat up straight. This season was *different* — that didn't mean it was *bad*. It was simply a new season in my life, like spring or fall — it would be what I made of it. The ball was in my court.

Shortly after the morning crew came in, patients started arriving. I'd been off for three days and maybe it was just Christmas, but my coworkers seemed a bit goofy today. We sent a little girl with appendicitis to surgery, a young woman who was eight months pregnant to women's center for observation after a car accident, called in the orthopedic doc for consult on a lawyer with a broken leg. I'd noticed one of the guys from the lab along with Katy from radiology off by the door — their heads together talking animatedly. I wondered if this was a new thing or not a thing at all. The season did have an affect on people.

Nicole and I were taking inventory during a little quiet spell. When we stood side by side she leaned towards me. "Mel, how were your days off?"

"Fine — great. I went to a concert. Other than that the usual writing, cleaning, baking, crossing things off lists. And you?"

"Oh, it's been good. My son will be off for Christmas so he'll be home. My folks are coming up from Anchorage to join us for a few days. Will you be alone?"

"I'm never alone. God is always with me."

"Yes, He is always with you, Mel. What are your plans? My church is doing the special Christmas Eve candlelight service again and you're invited. Sheila is coming too."

"Oh, good. Before she became the nursing supervisor we used to get together for dinner sometimes. Jack Frost loves her to pieces — she always brought treats for him and Snowball. It will be so nice to see her outside of work again. I figured she'd be going to Florida to see her kids."

"She said she's going in the spring this year."

"I don't know why my church doesn't do Christmas Eve services, but I really enjoyed coming to yours last year. It was already on my list. I have my afternoon and evening all planned out."

"Well, good. I'm so happy you'll be coming. I have to go early so I can save you a seat if you'd like."

"Please do." We went back to our work without any more conversation.

In the afternoon, Margie who worked in admissions came through with some papers for a patient to sign. On her way back out she stopped at the nurses station.

"Hey, Margie, so what are your plans for Christmas?" I asked.

She shrugged. "Did you know Cliff ran off with my friend? Some boyfriend he has been. On again, off again, begging me to come back to him just so he can break my heart again."

"Oh no, I'm so sorry."

She lifted her chin. "I don't need that loser or my so-called friend. I figure I'll just get a date with a good bottle of bourbon for Christmas Eve since I'm off on Christmas." She walked out of the ER.

After discharging a patient I noted the time. Admissions changed shift at five o'clock and that was two minutes away. I caught Grace and asked her to listen for the phone and went out to the admissions desk. "Margie, you're still here. Good, I want to ask you something."

CHAPTER 5

*M*argie pulled her purse out of her desk drawer and pushed her chair back. "What do you need? The night girl will be out in a sec."

"No, no I don't need admissions, I need to talk to you. I've known you since you and Leighton went to high school together. I know your folks divorced and you had a hard time, but I see you here at work doing an excellent job and I'm proud of you."

She tilted her head and her eyes looked watery. "Thank you, Mel. That's something I don't hear much."

I reached out to touch her arm. "Look, Margie, I'm alone this Christmas too but I'm not letting this special season escape me. Cancel your date with the bourbon and join me. I'll make us a nice steak dinner, we will go to a candlelight service then go home and watch a sappy Christmas movie. Then you can stay the night and go home whenever you want because I have to be here bright and early Christmas morning. I'd love to have you. My dog and cat would love the extra company too. Please say you'll come."

"I don't know — I'm not good company right now." She wiped a tear off of her face.

"You don't have to be good company, Margie. Just agree to come. Please?" I handed her a tissue from the box on the counter.

"I guess being with a mother figure would be a lot better than getting all sloshed over a loser."

"When you put it that way how can you refuse?" I smiled.

"Okay. Just let me know when and where."

I opened my arms to invite her to a hug. She hesitated a moment, looked around to make sure no one was looking and allowed me to give her a quick embrace.

"Great, I'm so happy you'll allow me to host you. You made my day." I nearly skipped back to the ER, my heart light. As I approached the desk, I noticed Katy with Skip, from the lab leaned over the counter talking to Grace. When I got close they got quiet. "So are we talking about Christmas surprises over here?"

Katy looked sheepish. "Well, maybe. You tell us."

I furrowed my brow. "What on earth are you talking about?"

Grace smiled like she knew something.

Katy held her phone out to me and I felt my face turn red. There was a photo of Dr. Fletcher and I having coffee with his hand over mine. I tried to remain calm. "Where did you get this?"

"Seems Miss 'I don't date' *does*?" She drawled out the last word. She looked like the Cheshire Cat, sitting there with a 'I just ate a yummy mouse' look."

"Oh for crying out loud, you guys. Don't you ever run into people you know in town? I was shopping for a book and then got myself a cup of coffee and Dr. Fletcher happened to be there too. Why would someone take a picture of us? And you are taking it totally out of context.

Oh! It was the phlebotomist. What's her name? Is it Bea? I saw her standing there texting like a banshee. So she's spreading rumors?" I took a breath and tried to calm down. Not only would I never have suspected someone would talk about me of all people — I mean I'm not one of the kids at work — I'm beyond being interesting to them. And I certainly didn't want Dr. Fletcher to hear about this. "Our meeting was completely innocent and coincidental. And why am I trying to explain myself to you?" I didn't know why I was so flustered, but it was about to get worse.

"Something big has happened and I'm the last to know? What's all the excitement?" I turned to see that Dr. Fletcher had come up behind me from the doctor's lounge. I turned Katy's phone off and put it in her hand — firmly. I had no idea how much he heard, but I hoped he hadn't seen anything. "Amelia, can I have a word with you?"

Oh, shoot. I got a sick feeling in my gut. Grace, Katy and Skip needed someone to wash the grins off their faces. I would have thrown them washcloths to do the job, but the supply closet wasn't on my way to the doctor's station. "What is it, Doc? You heard what they were talking about?"

"No, I wanted to ask you if the patient in room three got his prescription taken care of earlier?"

"Yes, he did and I talked to our social worker, Pam, and she was going to go to the pharmacy with him to make sure he got what he needed. Poor guy. At least he has an advocate now."

"Good and thank you for taking care of all of that. And what were the youngsters talking about that had you on the defense?"

It was frustrating having fair skin. Red is the first color people notice and it comes out so easily in my face. I could never be a poker player. "Nothing. You know how they are? Always looking for someone to tease."

He looked at his computer screen. "If you say so." Then he began to hum *Sleigh Ride*. I threw my hands up, walked away and began my end-of-shift room checks. What is it this time of year that makes people so weird?

The next two days it seemed people either hushed when I walked up or they gave me a goofy grin. Except Gil, who said, "Whoa momma! Go get 'em tiger."

"Gil, you of all people. You aren't a silly girl, you know better."

"But I saw the photo and it looks pretty obvious."

I put my hands on my hips. "You work in an ER. You know things aren't always as they seem." I threw my hands up and went to the locker room thankful that I didn't have to be back here for four days.

Friday evening I decided to wear my hair down. I slipped into my little black dress, and matching black dress boots before bundling up in a long wool coat, scarf and gloves for my drive to town. I was going to see the Nutcracker Ballet alone, but it was celebratory and I wanted to dress up and enjoy the evening. I parked and hurried inside to the warmth of the theater. I purchased my ticket at the entrance where some teens volunteers were checking coats. I handed mine over and put the claim check in my purse.

"Amelia, what a lovely surprise." I looked up to see Dr. Fletcher and his daughter checking their coats.

"This is a surprise." I scanned the near crowd to see if I knew anyone who might be taking misleading pictures of us with their cell phone.

He put his arm around his daughter. "Violet, I'm sure you've seen Amelia in the ER but you haven't been introduced. She's the one who spoils us with treats all the time."

I put out my hand. "Lovely to officially meet you, Violet. Your dad speaks highly of you. He's quite proud of his girls, but I imagine you already know that."

"It's nice to meet you, Amelia. Are you with someone?" She glanced around.

"No, I got released to go out solo, but I have my ankle monitor on under my boots." She looked puzzled.

Dr. Fletcher laughed. "Aside from bringing treats she brings an odd sense of humor to work too." He held out his arm. "Please, come sit with us."

I felt my fair skin betraying me once again as heat rose to my face. "Oh, no that's okay. You two enjoy the ballet."

Violet took her father's other arm. "Please join us. Dad wouldn't offer if he wasn't sincere." We took our seats, Mitch sitting between us ladies.

The ballet was delightful. I found it quite pleasant to sit with someone I knew and during intermission, Mitch brought Violet and I both a small glass of wine. We chatted and laughed and sampled some of the refreshments. At the end of the performance, we went to pick up our coats. "Thank you both for inviting me to sit with you. I loved the ballet, the dancers did an incredible job — and it was fun to enjoy it in your company."

"Would you care to go out for coffee with us?" Mitch asked.

"Oh no, but thank you for the invite. There's a timer on my ankle bracelet, you know." I winked and Violet laughed. I gave her a quick hug. "Hope you and your dad have a wonderful Christmas, Violet."

Mitch helped me with my coat then put his arm around my shoulder and gave me a squeeze before helping his daughter with her coat. I drove home singing, *It's the most wonderful time of the year.* Alaska waved her Northern Lights across the sky like a banner to accompany me. *Thank you, God for this most wonderful time of year.*

The next morning I followed my routine of caring for Jack Frost and Snowball, read my Bible and spent some time thanking God. I had so much to be thankful for. Mid morning I opened my laptop and found that I had email from Strike a Match. I opened the site and found dozens of responses to my profile. That couldn't be right. I opened the notifications. There were men who had 'favorited' me, and some who sent a 'smile' and a number of men had sent messages. I opened one from a man in Texas who had written, *'I like your picture. I'm a Christian too. How do you feel about nudist camps? My brother-in-law said I shouldn't ask that. What do you think?'*

I realized my mouth was hanging open and closed it with my hand. Initially I became angry and wanted to write him a piece of my mind. I called Angie. "You won't believe what some guy wrote to me and he claims he's a Christian," I raged. Angie laughed. "Why are you laughing?"

"Well, you said you were getting on the site to see how it works."

"Yes, but why would he write to me?"

"You are doing this to get fodder for a romantic comedy, right?"

"Yes, but..."

"It sounds like a good start. I imagine this is the sort of thing one has to wade through on dating sites. I think you're going to have some good material."

I took a deep breath and released it. "You're absolutely right, Ang. I took it personally and this isn't about me. I'm not looking to date." I thought of Mitch and got quiet.

"Are you still there? What's happening? Mel?"

I told her about running into Mitch at *The Book and Bean*, the picture floating around the hospital and the ballet.

"Ohh. This is getting interesting. And someone took pictures of you guys all snuggled up?"

"We were *not* snuggled up. It was an innocent moment

between friends and taken out of context. You know I don't date."

"If you did, what color would the date notebook be?" She giggled.

"Oh, you are just too funny. Have a great day, girl." We said goodbye and promised to talk soon.

I intended to be polite and answer each man with a standard reply; 'Thank you for considering my profile. I'm currently communicating with someone. Blessings on your search.' But I decided to ignore the nudist camp opportunity man.

Vacuuming and dusting sounded inviting by mid morning, so I turned up the 1940s' Christmas playlist and sang while I worked. I pulled the sheets out of the dryer and put them on my bed and sprayed a bit of lavender essential oil on my pillow so that hopefully when I went to bed I could sleep peacefully.

After sharing my lunch with Jack, I got out my red notebook. I had it divided into sections involving my move and opened to the one marked HOUSING. There was one more contractor I wanted to contact.

I had seen online some of the lovely Craftsman houses he built in communities and wanted to ask if he'd consider building a small cottage in one of his neighborhoods. I didn't need a big house to keep up and if I lived in a friendlier climate than Alaska I'd spend more time outdoors anyway.

I dialed and was surprised when the man answered his own phone. He was friendly and professional. He asked exactly what I had in mind and promised to email me a couple floor plans as soon as we were off the phone.

He also told me I could mark up changes and send them back and he could price them out for me. The ratings I found on him were all excellent and I was confident he'd build a home that I could enjoy and be proud of. I could hardly wait for the plans to come in so I could print them off and spend some time thinking about what I wanted.

I had been praying about which of the places I wanted to move to. One was Oregon and the other, Idaho. Although I didn't feel God leading specifically either way, I figured He would bless my move as long as I put Him first. I'd been through Oregon a number of times and knew some other people who had moved there from Alaska. Also I had been in Idaho to visit friends in Sun Valley. I don't ski so had gone in the summer. It was lovely, but in the end, Boise had more of the things on my list and housing was less expensive, so it made more sense for me. I got my scissors and cut out the Oregon section and ran it through the shredder. I would focus on Idaho.

That evening my phone rang. "Hey, Mom. How are you doing?"

"Tyson! It's so good to hear your voice, son. Where are you?"

"I'm in Germany. I met some folks who invited me to come for Christmas. There's a Christmas market here that you'd go nuts over." He laughed.

"I'm jealous. And I'm so glad you won't be alone for Christmas. How are you doing?" I didn't hear much from him. After his dad died, he was angry at his father, but had pulled away from me too, saying he needed to just go and figure things out. Figure out his father? Good luck with that.

"I"m doing okay, Mom. Time heals all wounds, they say."

"Do you believe that?"

"No, but I've had a lot of time to think, see things from different perspectives — and pray."

My heart leapt to hear him say he prayed. "I'm so glad. I pray for you and Leighton every day. I know how hard everything has been on you boys."

"I've had time to realize it was probably even harder on you. After all you were married to the guy."

A tear threatened to slide from my eye and even though he couldn't see me, I quickly wiped it away. "Do you have any plans to come to back to the states?"

"Actually, that's why I called. I've been talking to Leighton. He's quite the man. I figured he'd be angry with me because I left so soon after the funeral, but he's been really understanding. Or at least tries to be. Guess because he's a dad and an older brother he sees things I missed. Anyway, he and Jeannie invited me to come to Wyoming. I was wondering if maybe you could get away and come down for a visit sometime. I know they'd all love to see you."

"This sounds like an answer to prayer for me too. I've decided to leave Alaska. With all her allure, she's also harsh and unforgiving. I was thinking about flying to Boise to visit the hospitals there and get a feel for the city. I could easily rent a car and drive to Wyoming from there. Keep me posted and we'll make this happen. Thank you so much for calling."

"Wow, you are seriously thinking of leaving Alaska? Never thought I'd hear you say that."

"It's a new season of life, Ty."

"Merry Christmas, I love you, Mom."

"I love you, Tyson. Merry Christmas, honey."

Christmas Eve morning I woke up long before the sun, which considering it's only three days after the shortest day of the year isn't saying much. I stretched under my covers and Jack roused on his bed on the floor next to mine. He stuck his chin up on my bed and wagged his tail — slow and steady then increasing in speed and intensity. "Oh, okay, come on." He jumped on the bed, tried to lick my face and rolled onto his back, feet sticking up in the air and body wiggling. I reached over and rubbed his belly and his tongue hung out the side of his mouth.

"You are rotten," I said as I scratched his ear with the other hand. When I stopped he put his chin on my pillow and sighed. We lay there, the only light coming from the moon.

Thank you, Father, for this precious season. Thank you for my sons, friends, Jack and Snowball, a warm bed and food to eat.

I think of your Son being born in an unwelcoming world. I want to be deliberate about always having room in my heart for you. Let me be a light for you.

"Okay, Jack, up and at 'em. Today is Christmas Eve." I pushed the covers back and he stayed right where he was. I went down the hall and opened the bin to get his kibble when he immediately appeared. "Oh, the way to a guys heart is through his tummy, eh?" I scratched his ear.

After my usual morning chores I got my shower and put on a Contemporary Christian Christmas playlist.

I turned the Christmas lights on and started checking off todays list; veggies prepped for tonight, flourless chocolate cake in the oven, a goodie tray assembled to take to work tomorrow for the ER crew, and smaller ones for the holiday staff in housekeeping, lab and radiology. I put treats in stockings for Jack and Snowball and made up a stocking for Margie. I thought I would hang it up after she went to bed tonight and she'd find in the morning after I left for work.

At three thirty in the afternoon, I headed for town, making a quick stop at the house Leighton and Jeannie had lived in. I left the car running and scurried to the door and rang the bell. When the lady came to the door, I handed her a platter of cookies and candies laid out like a wreath around a balsam fir candle in the center. "Oh, what a surprise! But I don't have anything for you." She pulled her sweater around her neck with one hand.

"Merry Christmas! This isn't an exchange, just a little something to help you celebrate. It's been so cold I don't go out until I need to go to work, get groceries or appointments."

"Oh, we understand. We don't get out at all in this cold. This certainly isn't California."

"No, it's not. Quite a drastic change for you. Hope you get to spend enough time with your daughter's family to make it worth while. Will they be coming over?"

"Yes, they're going to bring the kids and spend the night tonight. We are looking forward to having them."

"Enjoy." I waved and scurried back to the car, shivering. Maybe my next car should have heated seats. Maybe my next car wouldn't need heated seats. I smiled. I wondered what possessed my neighbors to move to Alaska. She was a boom and bust land to treasure seekers. Gold diggers and oil riggers had trekked to her by the masses over the years, to take riches from her veins. Although she was gracious to some — others she made fools of — for thinking they could take advantage of her before she turned cold and unforgiving. Many men fought each other and even died in pursuit of her favor.

I had asked Margie to meet me at the hospital because it was on the way to the church where Christmas Eve service would be held. I saw her pull in the lot just ahead of me. Perfect timing. I pulled up behind her and she got in the passenger seat and looked straight ahead as I drove. "Are you okay?"

She sat with her arms wrapped around herself. "I'm cold and I'm hurt and I'm angry, but other than that, yeah, I'm okay." She glanced over at me and tried to smile but it didn't reach her eyes. "I've haven't gone into a church since I was a kid."

"I love it. There's just something special about it, but I'm not going to say much because your experience will be yours, not mine." We drove the next two miles noting businesses and homes lit up with the lights of the season. Their shine extra sparkly with the frost and snow and cold.

Nicole had saved seats in the second row for Sheila, Margie and me. I hoped that wouldn't be too uncomfortable for Margie. She seemed self-conscious at first but the lights were dimmed and the program started. A gentleman read part of the Christmas story from the Bible, while a young couple enacted a weary, pregnant Mary and an attentive Joseph traveling. A soloist sang, *Mary Did You Know*. The congregation sang a carol followed by more Scripture reading, and a woman did an interpretive dance. The program was an hour long. At the end a hush settled over the room when the lights were turned out, and a single candle flickered in the front of the church, its flame shared to ignite the candles held by congregants. Soon the room was bathed in the soft glow of candles as voices lifted singing, *Joy to the World*.

The lights were turned up again and candles distinguished. The atmosphere had decidedly changed. People greeted, hugged and wished others well. Nicole came over to us before we had moved out into the aisle. "I'm so glad you guys came. I hope it helps put you in the Christmas Spirit."

"I enjoyed it even more than last year, Nicole. A beautiful presentation that allowed everyone to participate, not just be observers." I hugged her. Margie's body language let people know she didn't want to be randomly hugged. Her wall had been built solidly years ago. We stopped in the foyer to get our coats and briefly chatted with people we recognized. An older man who I assumed to be the pastor of this church warmly greeted us, as did several women. They also invited us to attend one of their several Bible studies. Sheila came out and I invited her to come to my house. "I'd love to but

I'm going to another friend's tonight. Her husband just died and I don't want her to be alone."

"I'm sorry for her loss. I'm glad you can be there for her tonight — Merry Christmas."

"Merry Christmas to you, Mel. Give Jack and Snowball a kiss for me."

"I will." I waved and turned towards my car. We got in and I turned the heat up on high. "I have a quilt in the backseat, but it's as cold as the car. You can use it if you want though."

Margie looked straight ahead. "Actually, I'm cold, but I feel warm, if that makes any sense?"

"Yes, it does."

"I've never been to church at Christmas. And I've never been to anything like that before. It's like it kinda makes it real. I never thought about Jesus or his parents or angels or anything. Our Christmases were to get all excited about Santa, then Christmas morning dad would have a hangover and he and mom would yell at each other until one of them would go out slamming doors. Until they got divorced and mom was just bitter. By then I was old enough not to expect peace at home let alone on earth."

"It was a lovely service, wasn't it? I'm so glad you came and got to experience it. Now, I'm getting hungry. I have a couple of nice steaks waiting just for us."

"I'm looking forward to this dinner. You always bring good food to work, but steak — yum."

"Okay, we'll stop and get your car and you can follow me home to let the celebrating commence." I giggled.

She looked over at me and laughed. "You are good for me, Mel."

CHAPTER 6

*J*ack Frost and Snowball were ecstatic that I brought another pair of hands home to pet them. I went straight to the kitchen and started dinner. Music played in the living room and Margie who couldn't carry a tune made a joyful noise. I smiled as I spritzed the broccoli with olive oil, tossed it with pecans and stuck it in the oven to roast while I cooked the steaks. The twice baked potatoes heated in the microwave since I had prepared them earlier.

I whipped the whipping cream that we would have on our flourless chocolate cake for dessert, then crushed a candy cane and flaked some dark chocolate to sprinkle over the top. I opened the chilled sparkling cider and poured it into crystal goblets. The candles in the evergreen and rose center-piece were lit and the napkins folded and tucked into poin-settia napkin rings. Earlier I had set the table with my Christmas china. A bell shaped crystal bowl served as a relish tray. I mentally checked my list for dinner preparations. Assured that everything was ready, I stood in the doorway of the living room. "Okay, critters, you have to let Margie alone long enough to come eat."

Margie went to the bathroom to wash her hands then walked into the dining room. She stopped and seemed to be taking it in. "Oh wow, it looks like you're expecting someone special. This is beautiful. I'm used to eating on the couch in front of the television. Food that comes from the gas station usually."

"Yes, someone special is here. Come, sit down."

I served the steaks and vegetables and sat down across from Margie.

"Um, is someone else coming?" She nodded to the setting at the head of the table.

"Call me weird. I set a place to remember why I can celebrate. It's at the head of the table because Jesus is the head of my life. It's symbolic to welcome Him. And to remember to thank Him."

She nodded. I thanked God for the meal, the season, and for sending Margie to share it with, and then we chatted while we ate. We both had leftovers to eat the next day — Christmas Day. I put hers in a plastic container with a lid, and told her if she didn't eat it for breakfast, not to forget to take it home with her. We did the dishes together then put on pajamas and turned on a Christmas movie. About fifteen minutes into the movie, her phone chimed. She looked at it and immediately tensed. "It's *him*. He says he wants to talk."

I paused the movie. "Do you want to talk to him?"

She shrugged. "I don't know."

I turned on the sofa to face her. "How have you felt this evening?"

"What? I feel good. Actually I have felt really peaceful and happy."

"How does hearing from him make you feel?"

She hugged a throw pillow to her chest and then reached

over to pet Snowball. "Like I just had a car accident, anxious. Angry!"

"One more question. Is being with him where you want to be in ten or fifteen years?"

"Oh my stars, no!" She looked at me. "What have I been doing? Why have I wasted so much time with that creep?"

"Maybe he's what you thought you deserved? It was familiar? Only you can answer that question, Margie."

She opened her phone and concentrated on it for a bit then set it down and smiled. "I just blocked him. He wanted out. I'm finished. Is there more of that sparkling cider? I think we need to celebrate."

I brought the cider to the living room along with two goblets and she made a toast to new beginnings. She held her goblet and said, "Speaking of new beginnings — what about you and Dr. Fletcher?"

Thankful I hadn't just taken a drink to choke on or spray out my nose, I answered, "There is no 'about' with me and Dr. Fletcher. We simply ran into each other at *The Book and Bean* and chatted over coffee." I smiled confidently.

"But I heard someone saw you at the ballet with him and his daughter like a perfect little family."

I set my glass down and groaned. "This is not a big town. I never go anywhere without running into people I know. Again, it was just a chance meeting, and we ended up sitting together — that's *all*."

"Well, if that's true then it's kinda sad. Because everyone thinks you two would be perfect together. You're both upbeat and positive and care about other people. And besides that everyone thinks you guys look really cute together." She giggled.

"Why is *everyone* thinking about us at all? Looking cute together isn't enough to base a relationship on, Margie. Dr. Fletcher and I aren't traveling the same highway."

"Huh?"

"I'm moving in a matter of months. I made my decision after much debate and nothing is going to change that. I've listed all the pros and cons I can think of and moving wins. And I am serious about my relationship with God and if I ever considered being in a relationship, it would have to be with a man who is like minded."

"Maybe I should decide what I want in a relationship. I seem to gravitate to guys who pretend to like me as I am as long as I don't rock the boat. I never thought about them having any qualifications. I like that though. I can see where it might eliminate some of the losers."

Sleep overtook me while I prayed that Margie would see her own worth and I woke up at four in the morning. I'd always been an early riser and rather stealth, so I didn't worry about waking Margie. I could hear her softly snoring when I went by the guest room door and smiled that she sounded peaceful. I loaded up the goodies for work and left the house in the dark of the early Christmas morning. I drove to work singing along with Selah's *Rose of Bethlehem* album. The trees glistened as my car lights hit them. Winter — short days and long nights, but Alaska displayed her beauty even in the dark — majestic and powerful as a reigning queen. As long as you showed her respect, she was generous.

Every person working in the ER on Christmas Day had signed up to work the holiday so everyone seemed to be in good spirits. An occasional patient arrived giving us purpose. A frail elderly woman — influenza — admitted. A middle aged man — salmon bone caught in his throat — extracted. An inebriate found passed out in town on the sidewalk — wrapped in warm blankets and put in a room to sleep it off, then given a ride home. There had been no big catastrophes today. *Thank God.*

During one of the quiet spells, we gathered at the nurses station and shared Christmas treats. Josh said, "So did Margie come to your house last night?"

"Yes, I'm so glad she did. I really enjoyed spending time with her."

Dr. Fletcher said, "You're such a mom, Amelia."

I laughed. "Well, yes, I am a mom."

"I mean you have a mother's heart. We see it here. Like the time last fall when the State Troopers brought in the young woman who was about eight months pregnant."

I sighed. "I wonder how she's doing now and where her baby is."

"I wasn't here," Sophie said. "What happened?"

My hair was slipping from the scrunchy, so I rolled it back up and wrapped the scrunchy around it. "She had a huge void in her life."

Dr. Fletcher looked over at me and gave me a warm smile. "Amelia asked her why she was running from the police and if this was who she'd dreamed of being when she grew up."

"I remember that. I was going into the room with a bag of saline and Mel was *praying* with her. I told her I heard her praying in there." Josh laughed.

"So did I make a believer out of you yet, Josh?" I asked.

"You did make me think. But I wouldn't go that far. I'm not praying over patients."

"*Yet.*" I winked at him. "There's hope for you *yet.*"

Josh laughed and his face reddened. He leaned back, put his foot on the leg of my rolling chair and gave it a little shove.

Later while I rechecked inventory in a room we had used, my phone beeped. When I first started nursing it was against the rules to have a phone. Now we were required to have one as most of the doctors on call preferred to be reached by text messaging. I looked at my phone and saw that it was Margie. Since we had no patients I answered in case she was at the house and needed something. "Hey, what's up?"

"I know you're at work so will keep it short but I'm going to head home in a little bit. I've been lounging around your house enjoying the company of Jack Frost and Snowball. It's so peaceful here that I not only slept — I slept until almost ten o'clock. And thank you for the stocking! That was a fun surprise. I feel like a kid."

"I'm glad to hear that. Do you need anything? You know you can stay as long as you like."

"No, I'm going to go home, but wanted to know if I can do anything before I leave? The place is so orderly I don't see anything that needs to be done, but feel like I should do something."

Dr. Fletcher came in the room. "Amelia, I just wanted to tell you how much Violet and I enjoyed being able to watch the ballet with you and — oh, I'm sorry. I didn't see you were on the phone. Talk to me when you're done." He slipped out.

I hoped Margie hadn't heard him. "Sorry Margie, someone came in to speak to me. You don't need to do a thing."

"I heard Dr. Fletcher's voice. Mel! You were just saying last night that there is no *about with* you and Dr. Fletcher. Does *he* know that? So are you reconsidering moving?"

Frustration blanketed me. "Margie, again, there is nothing going on. I'm moving. Why won't people give up on the match making and hear me?"

"Maybe we like the idea of happy ever after endings." She giggled.

"You're cute, Margie, very cute. Now get off the phone, I'm at work. Talk to you later."

I found Dr. Fletcher at his computer. He looked up and

smiled when I approached. "Violet was taken with you. She said she thought you were funny."

"She's a lovely young woman. You can be proud, Doc." I smiled.

"Yes, and she has a good head on her shoulders too." He smiled more to himself than me. "She and I are leaving for Colorado tomorrow night. We're going on a ski trip. Do you ski?"

"No, not snow skiing anyway. But I love to water ski."

"Water ski? And you're from Alaska?"

"A friend taught me when I was sixteen-years-old. We were on the lake at two o'clock in the morning when it wouldn't be so busy and stayed out there until after four o'clock. I loved it. And I didn't get frostbitten either." I grinned. "I'm going to do a walk through while things are quiet — see if I can find any little jobs to stay busy."

He seemed like his mind was far off, but he nodded.

I went through the department making notes of anything that should be ordered tomorrow, and then tidied things up. Each person seemed to have their own method of putting supplies away and by the looks of it, some of them probably cleaned their homes by stuffing everything under a bed or in the closet.

Some people call me a neat freak, but organization makes life easier. A life organized is a life in control. Organization made me feel more at peace in my world.

"Hey Mel?" Josh came up behind me.

I jumped. "Yes, what do you need?"

"The picture of you and Doc Fletcher — I know you said nothing is going on but he had his hand on yours and was leaning over talking to you. It sure looked like more than you say. Are you just trying to keep things quiet? Do you really like him? Personally I think you should let your hair down, *mom*." He smiled and reminded me of my own sons when they were small and trying to talk me into going for ice cream.

"Josh, honey — don't you have some work to do?" I shooed him away and went back to my work. But now my thoughts weren't on what I was doing. *Mitch is a really sweet man. Everyone likes him. He treats me well, but that's his standard for how he treats everyone. Of course I like him, but — and why did he ask me if I ski?*

At the end of shift a few patients came in with minor issues for the most part. Things that might not be minor if they had to wait to get in to a doctor's office. The day had been surreally peaceful and the crew interacted with a warm intimacy like a close family. I hugged Sophie and Josh at the end of the shift and wished the others a Merry Christmas. On the drive home I shivered on the outside, but a peaceful warmth flowed through me.

The next few days I wasn't scheduled to work in the ER, but I had many other things to work on. I reorganized my file of financial advising class materials. The company sent everything I needed, but I enjoyed adding my own touch to the class and watched for pictures, comics and stories that related to financial trials and victories that I could share to encourage my students.

The day before the class was to start, Sonya, one of the nurses who worked in ICU came to the ER looking for me.

"Mel, I know you're doing a financial class but with my schedule I can't make it. My manager told me she and her husband took it from you last year and they are out of debt.

"Yes, usually people are out of debt within eighteen months."

She pulled me away from listening ears. "I'm desperate. I've buried myself and now each time I get paid, I'm depressed because there's never enough to pay on all my debt."

I nodded. "I'm listening."

"Last year I bought a house, then a snow machine and then some other 'Alaska toys'. Then I had to have a garage built to hold all the toys. I'm going to lose everything if I can't find a way out of this."

"It sounds like you are ready to make some necessary changes, Sonya."

"Oh believe me, I am. Please help me."

"Can you meet me in town tomorrow? I'll bring you a book. You will have to pay for the book because I need to know you're serious enough to invest to get out of debt."

"How much is it? I'll get the money right now."

I wrote down the cost of the book and my phone number and handed it to her. "You're going to do fine. I'll meet you tomorrow and then you can call me with any questions or even if you just need encouragement. I'll also write my email address in the book. You can do this, Sonya."

She hugged me. "Thank you so much. I haven't even been able to sleep with all my worrying."

With the holiday celebrations, work, and getting ready for my class, I hadn't done much with my writing. To get back on track I pulled out my blue notebook and opened my laptop. I needed to check Strike A Match, but wasn't prepared to find so many hits on my profile. *Seriously? Are there really that many men looking for someone?* I figured everyone would be too busy for this stuff over the holidays. But then again if they're lonely they might spend even more time trying to find someone. As the first time, a lot of the hits were 'favorite' or 'smiles' but there were more messages than I wanted to spend the time reading just then. I deleted all the 'favorites' and 'smiles' before I went to the kitchen to make a brain freeze. This was going to take a while.

Harry wrote; *Hey doll. I'm a tennis and golf instructor, 45 years old, have one son in college. I'm looking for a faithful woman who enjoys sports, sporting events, watching sports and having a good time. Oh, I'm a Christian too.*

I copied and pasted my response to Harry and then to several more. I felt cross-eyed by the time I made it through the messages. I didn't want to read them all but didn't want to miss any little gems that I could potentially use in my book either. One thing I don't enjoy about writing is that it takes a lot of research time, so after a few hours I decided to hide my profile to allow time to catch up. I spent the next hour and a half making notes in the blue notebook under various categories before I had to stop and make myself something to eat — and spend some time with the critters.

January arrived under the weight of Alaska's coat of bitter cold. Alaska could paint her winter skies with the soft, baby blanket colors of blue, pink, yellow and peach, deceptively innocent and inviting, disguising her true harsh nature. Those who lived with her any length of time learned to tell her how beautiful she was, while respecting the fact that her nature was not always beautifully tempered. How she loved to be admired, yet wisdom dictated that she be respected most of all.

While on my way to work one dark morning, I saw tail-lights ahead and suddenly they swerved and hopped the edge of the road. I slowed my car then pulled over to the shoulder and stopped, turning my car so that my lights aimed the direction of the vehicle in distress. I flipped my emergency flashers on and stepped out of my car to investigate. I heard a soft moan and turned toward the passenger side. I spotted a young woman lying in the snow. I trudged through the snow to her. "Where are you hurt?" I squatted down and reached for her wrist to feel her pulse.

"I don't know. My back, I think." She moaned again. A quick observation proved she wasn't dressed for this weather. She was wearing a jacket, mid calf length stretch pants and flat shoes. Her pulse was fast, but she was breathing okay.

I stood up and looked for the driver. I found him still in the car, conscious, but unable to get out. "I took his pulse and looked for visible injuries. "Are you hurt?"

"My leg hurts. I'm not sure what happened. Maybe I hit a slick spot?" I smelled alcohol on his breath.

I patted his shoulder. "Just stay put for now, okay? I'm going to check on the girl. Is she a relative?"

"Nah, we were just at a party."

"Must have been quite a party."

A pickup truck approached and slowed. I waved it down. "Can you call 9-1-1? Two people involved, both conscious. Looks like the girl was thrown from the car."

The man in the truck said, "Do you need help?"

"I'm a nurse. After you get ahold of 9-1-1 you could come stay with the driver to make sure he stays alert — if you don't mind."

He gave me a thumbs up as he dialed his phone. I went back through the snow to the girl. She shivered uncontrollably — cold, but maybe shock too.

I pulled mittens out of my pocket and put them over her feet then unzipped my parka and lay down on the ground next to her. I pulled my left arm out of the parka sleeve and wrapped my parka over her, trying to warm her with the warmth of my own body. She whimpered. "I'm so scared."

"Are you scared because of the accident or because of your pain?"

"I wasn't supposed to be out and now this happened."

I held her, trying to comfort her. "I guess you are scared, but right now let's concentrate on first things first. Help is coming and you will get medical care, the rest can wait until later." As I spoke to her, she began to sob. "What's your name, honey?

"Heather. Please don't leave me, okay?"

"I'm not going anywhere, Heather. Can I pray with you?"

She sniffled. "I guess. I mean yes."

"Father," a wave of gratefulness fell over me as I looked up into the night sky and knew that God had put me at this place and at this time for His purpose. "Nothing is hidden from you. Even now you see Heather and you love her. Please let her keenly sense your presence and your love right now. Help her to know that she is never alone and even last night while she made poor choices, you didn't remove yourself. You were here to hold her and comfort her. Thank you for choosing me to be your arms. In Jesus' name, Amen."

I put my head next to hers while she wept. I could feel her tears as they froze on my cheek.

"When I was little I went to church. Then my mom died and when I went to a foster home. I guess I was just mad at God."

"He's big enough to handle our anger and hurt, Heather. I'm sorry you lost your mom. I understand how much that hurts. I lost mine too. Sometimes life isn't kind, but that doesn't mean that God stopped loving you."

We heard the siren of the ambulance approaching. Heather grabbed my hand. "Please don't leave me. Will you go with me?"

"You bet I will, but I won't be in the ambulance with you. I will follow though and I'll be with you at the hospital. Okay?

"You promise?"

"I promise. I gave a quick report to the paramedic and

EMT's as they loaded Heather into the ambulance. Dan was the paramedic.

He gave me a thumbs up. "Thank you, Mel. See you there."

When Heather noticed Dan, I knew she was taking in his size and good looks before she glanced at me, eyes large and round. I winked at her and she smiled. *She's not too hurt to appreciate the real estate.* I chuckled to myself.

The second ambulance crew loaded up the driver who didn't seem to be hurt enough that he couldn't walk, but they put him on a gurney for transport anyway. I thanked the truck driver who had stopped to help and got in my car to follow the ambulance that had taken Heather.

The ER social worker, Pam, had contacted the family Heather was staying with. The mom showed up to take Heather home and found me at the nurses' station.

"Heather asked me if I could get your phone number. She said you stayed with her this morning. Thank you for praying with her. She has been a mess since her mom died. I never should have let her go out last night. She was supposed to be back by ten o'clock."

I reached out to touch her arm. "I think the young man she was with had some influence on that decision. He's okay so hopefully he will arrive at the fact that he made some bonehead decisions that could have turned out much worse."

She gave me a quick hug. "I'm so glad you were there."

"I'm glad you were there for her when her mom died. Maybe she will see a pattern here of being loved even in hard circumstances." I'll stop by her room to say goodbye on my way to the pharmacy.

CHAPTER 7

*M*ost nights sleep came eventually, even if fitfully. But tonight my pillow was damp from my tears. It had been over three years since Jeff died, but I still felt the ache of betrayal sometimes. *Lord, sometimes I feel so lonely. I have felt that way for years. I know you will never leave me, but I long for someone I can share my heart with. Would you send me a friend? I'm sorry. I know your grace is sufficient, but in my flesh I crave companionship. Will you bring a true friend into my life? You know I'm not looking for love. Another woman who needs to be and have a friend would be fine. I had Angie, but now she's over two thousand miles away. I'd just like someone to talk to and maybe go for hikes or to a movie with. I'm surrounded by people, but I feel like an island.*

The clock told me that morning had arrived, but the darkness of winter masked her light. I got out of bed and automatically went through my morning routine. I turned on an instrumental worship playlist and went to my office and opened my laptop. There was a message from a guy named Tony.

Hey, beautiful. I go to church a couple times a year. I'm a retired lawyer from Minnesota who moved to Arizona for year round play time. I have a four wheeler, ski boat, motorcycle, convertible, a home with a view and a gourmet kitchen. If you're looking for a fun guy with all the toys, I just might be the man of your dreams.

Okay! A guy in his second childhood. FUN. NOT. I copied his note and pasted it into a file for my book. I wouldn't use these guys names or location, but what they wrote to me was fair game as far as I was concerned. And I wasn't certain his name was really Tony. After all, my name wasn't really Crystal, but that's what showed on my profile.

I decided to change my location on the site from Arizona to Montana.

I'd considered putting in Idaho, but I didn't want to end up moving and run into someone that had seen me online. Not that Montana would offer many hits on the site, but I could change the location again in a month.

Cabin fever repeatedly knocked on the door throughout the month. After the activities of December, January seemed to hold me prisoner. I went to work, and taught my financial advising class one evening a week. Other than that I didn't leave the house. I got groceries on the way home from work so I wouldn't have to make a trip into town.

Jack Frost was suffering from captivity as well. He moped around the house and sighed. "I'm sorry, Jack, I know how you feel. I have an idea." I grabbed one of his toys and shook it in the air. "Jack, sit." He sat. "Stay." He stayed. I held my hand up to keep him there while I snuck into my office and hid the toy. I came back to the living room. "Jack, search." Snowball remained on her perch on the sofa feigning disinterest, tail twitching.

Jack wiggled all over and took off to find his toy. He passed my office. "You're getting colder, Jack." He turned and stopped at the office door. "You're getting warmer." He cocked his head at me, wagged his tail and bolted into the office. His nose twitched in anticipation and then he stopped and held still — aside from his tail that swayed his whole back end. "Good boy, you found it!" I scratched his ear and said, "Do you want to try again?" He sat down, cocked his head and wagged his tail. "Okay, stay." I hid the toy in the pantry and partially closed the door. We spent the next half hour playing hot and cold before taking a break. I gave him a treat and he plopped on his bed in front of the fire to enjoy it.

"Do you feel better now?" He wagged the tip of his tail. "So do I." Snowball left her perch on the sofa to lie next to Jack Frost on his bed. He licked her head and she purred as she stretched then nuzzled up under his chin. He raised his eyebrows and looked at me. "Isn't it nice to be loved, Jack?" He sighed and closed his eyes.

While the critters took a winter's nap, I went to my office where the notes on my desk had become unruly. I couldn't think about writing until I had it organized, so I placed all the sticky notes in my blue notebook according to category, and then went to work on my outline. After a break I checked my profile on Strike a Match. Already there were messages including one from Bob, a park ranger in Wyoming.

Good morning, Crystal. I found your profile refreshingly honest. Most I have read on here seem superficial to me. I see that you are a widow and I can relate because I lost my wife four years ago. It's hard to meet people working as a ranger except during tourist season and they are here for the fair weather. Not many women want to live in a remote area and brave the lonely winters. I see you are in Montana, not too awfully far away, but imagine a woman like you lives in and appreciates the city. If you ever feel adventurous, you are welcome to write me. I'd love to meet you.

I copied and pasted my reply and for the first time I felt a little guilty. But Bob was right, I wasn't interested in Bob or winters in Wyoming in a remote location.

And the only adventure I wanted was to move to Boise and settle into a nice little cottage, and go to a job I enjoyed — where I could serve God using the talents and skills He'd given me.

That evening I made my decision. I called Robert Ide, realtor extraordinaire — at least that's what he told me when he gave me his card in the ER a couple months ago. He'd come in with indigestion that turned out to be gallstones and required surgery. Once we had him comfortable before he went to surgery, he became chatty and infatuated with the woman who dispensed the pain meds — me. He gave me his card and told me he'd give me a discount on his fee if I ever wanted to buy or sell a house. He also offered his hand in marriage. I was sure he wouldn't remember that part. Most of them didn't. I didn't keep the card, but I remembered him so looked up his number. The phone rang twice. "Hello, you have reached Robert Ide."

I waited a few seconds thinking I'd gotten a recording. "Hello?"

"Hello, this is Robert."

"I'm sorry, I thought you were a recording. My name is Amelia Montgomery and I would like to list my house for sale."

"Great, I'm your man. How did you hear about me, Amelia?"

"Actually we met in the ER a while back. I was your nurse."

"Mel?"

"Yes, that's me."

"Oh I remember you well. You took such good care of me. I really appreciated it. Now maybe I can serve you as well as you cared for me. Why don't you give me your address and tell me what's the best time for me to come do a walk through. I will tell you this isn't the hot market season — but we can get all the ducks in a row."

We set up a time for him to come and after we hung up I ran to the living room, sat on the chair and bounced up and down.

"Jack! Snowflake! We're going to do it! We will sell the house and move. Can you believe it? Oh, we have so much to do. Well, not you guys — you just be yourselves, but I have so much to do." I scanned the room.

"I guess it's not too early to sort things to pack is it? Never mind, I don't honestly expect you to answer that." I laughed. "Never mind me — I'm just excited. We're moving. Yay!"

That night I tossed and turned thinking about everything that would have to happen next. I had to start another list — things I had to do before Robert put the house on the market. And maybe a list of things I would give away. I thought I might need to buy another notebook. I finally got up around three o'clock because my mind wasn't interested in settling down and sleeping with my body. In my excitement I decided to call my travel agent and book a ticket to Idaho to start things rolling at that end. I could book my own tickets, but she'd done all my trips for years and did a good job. One less thing I had to worry about. Oh, but I couldn't call her at three thirty in the morning. Well, I put her on the top of a new list. Above that I wrote a note to put in for a few days off work to make the trip. I grabbed a new sticky note to rewrite the list — I couldn't tolerate messy lists.

With Valentine's Day around the corner, I stopped at the store to pick up cards to send to my grandkids. They weren't small anymore, but they enjoyed the silly cards with small gift cards stuck inside. Next I stopped at *The Book and Bean* and ran into Nicole, and then Katy from work. We chatted as we stood in line for coffee and I decided to take one of the tables to sip my drink and get the cards ready to mail while the other two went to browse the store. A chair pulled out behind me. "Mind if I sit here?"

Oh, no. "Um, that's fine Dr. — I mean Mitch. So we meet again."

He pulled the chair close to the table. "Sending a Valentine to someone special?" he asked.

"Yes, my grandkids."

"Ah. You have two sons and how many grandkids?"

"Leighton, my older son has three kids. Tyson is still foot-loose." I smiled.

"I always pictured myself with a son or two to raise, but I do love my daughters."

"I'm sure you do. They will always need you, but sons grow up and make their own lives. Not that girls can't be independent."

"With Violet making plans to move away soon, I find myself rethinking things a bit." He looked down and played with his coffee cup. "Of course Rose graduated from college three years ago, but I wasn't ready for Violet to be gone yet. Seems like it happened so fast."

"I know what you mean. You raise them to make their own way in life and then when they do, they leave a void. You ponder what's next. I know I'm ready to make some big changes."

"Such as moving?"

I rubbed my temples. "Yes"

"I'm sure you've thought this all out since you live by lists, but can I ask when, where, how?"

I chuckled. "Well, detective — I hope to move as soon as winter ends and the roads are clear. It will be hard to leave in the summer but I certainly don't want to tackle it alone in the winter. I've driven the highway before, but not carrying my household. The where — I have whittled that list down to Boise, Idaho. The how — that part I'm still working on. Moving companies charge an arm and a leg and there's no guarantee that my furniture would still be in good shape when it arrived." I took a sip of my drink. "So there's always the option of renting a truck and moving myself."

"That could work. I know there are plenty of people who would come help you load the truck — including me." He reached out and touched my arm above my wrist. "You have goosebumps. Is that from your drink?"

Goosebumps ran all the way up my arm at his touch, and once again I felt my face burning. Was this conversation getting personal or was it just me? I cleared my throat and folded my hands in my lap. "One challenge to that plan — I don't know anyone where I'm looking at moving. So how would I unload the big stuff? I haven't gotten it all figured out yet." I looked down at my drink and for some reason I looked at Mitch and blurted, "Want to know a secret? I called my travel agent to look at tickets last night."

"You did? For what?"

"I'm going to go check out the hospitals and meet with a contractor about a house. Actually I have another secret — I just put my house on the market. Signed a contract with Robert Ide — remember him?"

"Wow, so this is really going to happen for you? I guess I'm happy for you, if that's what you want. There's good skiing in Idaho too." He leaned back in his chair and smiled.

"I have to make sure I can take a few days off work before I buy the tickets. I'm going to go by and check on my way home. I suppose I should run over to the post office first and get these cards mailed. It's always nice to see you. Have a good rest of your day." I stood up and gathered my things into my bag and picked up my cup to toss it in the trash.

Mitch stood up and took my cup from me. "So what are your plans for the evening?"

A rush of confusion blew through me. I hoped he wasn't about to ask me out. I can't date him. I pulled on my coat. "When I'm done in town I'm going home to spend some time working on my book. I hope you have a nice evening with Violet. Enjoy it while you can."

"Actually I'm going to work this evening. I'll have dinner with her, then work the midnight shift tonight. See you soon, Mel?"

"Yes, of course, I'm working this weekend." Again my face reddened. Why did I think he was going to ask me out? I got all freaked out about nothing. As I left the store I saw Katy sitting in her car talking on her phone. I waved and she grinned but looked past me. I glanced back and saw Mitch leaving right behind me heading the same direction in the parking lot. *Oh great, more fodder for the rumor mill.*

I mailed my cards and was walking out of the post office when my phone rang. I pulled it out of my coat pocket and had to take my glove off to answer it. I missed a step and cruised most ungraciously down the remaining steps to the curb. Pain exploded in my ankle and sent shock waves through my body.

Okay, I'm an ER nurse, I can handle this. Stay calm, breathe deep, make a plan. My bag had landed just out of my reach and my phone had skidded under a parked car. 'Okay, God, this is one of those times I need your help.' I tried to stand up but my ankle wasn't buying it. *'God, I think I need your help right away. How could I be so stupid? I know it's icy out here. And this is embarrassing.'* It hurt my vanity to consider that someone would see me lying there in the parking lot. Shortly a lady came out, and I saw her look at me.

"What on earth are you doing down there?" She asked as though I were a child.

"I'm trying to reach my phone." I looked up and knew my smile was more of a grimace.

"Well, you should watch yourself. You could get hurt out here on the ground."

Or I could get hurt by the ground. I pointed toward my bag. "Would you be so kind as to hand me that bag?"

She turned to look where I was pointing and shrugged. "Here you go. And you really need to get up before you trip someone."

"Yes, ma'am. Thank you." She walked away and I knew I could have asked her for help but I wasn't convinced she could do anything for me. The pain in my ankle throbbed again now that I wasn't distracted. I got down on my belly and crawled to reach my phone under the car and just before I could reach it, I heard a police siren.

A moment later, from my viewpoint I saw boots walking my direction before they stopped on the other side of the car. Then I saw knees on the ground followed by a face peering under the car.

"Is this your car, lady? I noticed you crawling around. It's kind of cold and you could get hurt in a parking lot like that. Someone might not see you and run over you."

The boots walked around the car to where I was sprawled on the ice and I pushed myself backwards from under the car. "I dropped my phone and I'm trying to reach it."

"Well, stand up here and I'll get it for you."

"That's a bit of a problem right now, officer. I'm not sure I can stand up."

"Oh, I know it's getting dark out, but it's not even evening. A little early to be hitting the sauce, isn't it? Maybe we need to do a Breathalyzer test?"

My ankle felt like it was growing to the size of a large onion. "Sir, I have *not* been drinking. I slipped and my bag went one way and my phone went another as I was coming out of the post office." Anger began to compete with pain and then I got a look at the officer's face. He frequently came to the ER on police business. "Bill! For crying out loud, you know me and you know I wouldn't be falling down drunk!"

He actually looked at my face then. "Mel! Wow, what happened to you? Are you hurt? Do you want me to call an ambulance?"

"No, I want you to help me get my phone and then help me stand up. Please?"

"Ah man, I'm so sorry." He leaned down and was able to reach my phone and handed it to me. I dropped it into my bag. He helped me up. "Are you okay? You sure you don't want me to call an ambulance?"

At the thought of an ambulance, Dan came into my mind and I smiled. "No, but thank you. I'm sure it's a little sprained and I know what to do for it." Humiliated and embarrassed, I gingerly hopped on the ice on my good foot to my car. At least it was my left ankle that I'd hurt, so I could still drive. *God, thank you for sending me help. Now if I can just get home, I'll ice and elevate it.*

By the time I got home, took care of the critters and got my leg up, my ankle felt like a cantaloupe. A blue cantaloupe. I had taken an ibuprofen, and had ice on it but I'd never had a pain like this from a sprain before. In fact it was enough pain that I remained on the sofa watching movies until after midnight. Feeling a little goofy from lack of sleep and no lack of pain, I picked up my phone and took a picture of my ankle.

Then being silly I texted it to Gil who would be working ER tonight, with the caption, 'think I need an x-ray?'. Two minutes later my phone rang.

"Hello?"

"Amelia, this is Mitch. Gil shared the picture with me.

Where are you? When did this happen? How did it happen? Why didn't you call me? I told you I was working tonight."

"Um — I'm at home. At the post office after I left you. I slipped on the steps. I know how to treat a sprain."

"Okay, well that doesn't look like a simple sprain to me. You need to be seen."

"I had planned to come by the hospital to ask about my time off, but my ankle hurt so I came home. I took an ibuprofen and I have it iced and elevated. If it's still bad in the morning, I will come in. Okay?"

"I'll be concerned about you all through my shift."

I laughed. "Thank you, Mitch. But be concerned for your real patients. Have a good night." I hung up and in spite of the ice on my ankle, there was a warmth in my core that someone was concerned for me. No, that Mitch was concerned for me. And that confused me. Mitch is a good man and a caring doctor — but I can't go there. I. Don't. Date.

By seven thirty in the morning, my ankle felt worse, if anything. I'd hardly been able to sleep aside from little dozes. Each one ended with scenes of me being run over in the post office parking lot and a woman standing over me telling me I was bad and wouldn't be getting any Valentines. I hobbled to the shower, dried off and pulled on stretch pants that flared at the ankle. I had to find my big wool socks as the everyday socks weren't going to cover that ankle. I fed the critters and as much as I hated to, I got ready to drive to the hospital. Before I could get my boots on, my phone alerted me to a message. GOOD MORNING AMELIA. I'M NOT LEAVING HERE UNTIL YOU COME IN AND HAVE THAT ANKLE LOOKED AT. MITCH

I texted back, 'blah blah blah Stop YELLING. I'm on my way.'

The drive was challenging, mostly due to the pain. I

couldn't get my ankle in a comfortable position. But twenty minutes later I arrived and parked as close as I could to the door without being illegally parked. When I got out of the car, I slipped — warm boot sole on ice — but caught myself on my car. I texted, "I'm here," and within seconds, Gil came running through the door with a wheelchair. *Oh great I get to make a big scene. Arghh.*

He wheeled me inside and Ellen and Dr. Fletcher followed us into a patient room. Before Josh could help me stand up, Mitch scooped me up onto the stretcher.

"You'll hurt your back," I protested.

"Not lifting you, I won't. Which ankle is it?"

"Left."

Ellen pulled off my boot and made a face. "Oh, Mel, you're not running away on that."

"Tell me about it. It happened so fast and I knew I hurt it, because the pain differed from any I've felt before. But I didn't feel like spending my evening here."

Dr. Fletcher said, "It's hurts us that you preferred to be home rather than in our company." He winked. "I'm ordering x-rays now — three view and a CT — we'll see what needs to be done. Do you need something for pain?"

"No, I don't, thank you. Don't make a fuss over me, guys. I'm one of you."

Josh brought me a blanket from the warmer oven and wrapped it around my shoulders. Margie put an ID bracelet on me and Ellen offered me something for pain again, which I turned down. "Wow, no wonder people come here. This is better than the Hilton." I grinned. "Thank you guys for taking such good care of me."

Josh hugged me and said, "Well, Mom, you always take good care of us." He grinned.

Margie said, "Yes you do. And it means a lot. Now it's our turn." She came around and hugged me too. I knew that she wasn't much into hugging, so I didn't miss the significance of her action. "I love you kids, you know that? Now get back to work." I waved my hand to shoo them out the door.

~

As I tossed in my bed that night, ankle elevated and Jack Frost nudging my hand repeatedly for assurance that everything was okay, I alternately berated myself for getting hurt and feeling silly because how could I have made the ice not slippery? I just hated being forced to be off work with an injury. I did break my ankle, but it was clean so no surgery had been required. That in itself I counted as a blessing. Frustration and pain competed for my energy until sometime in the wee hours of the morning when sleep shut them both down.

Morning arrived and somewhat impaired by my swollen ankle, the bulky walker boot, and crutches that Mitch had prescribed — I limped through my normal routine before taking an ibuprofen with my brain freeze. It hit me that this didn't have to be wasted time off work, but in fact it could be an opportunity to work on my book.

Feeling energized at the prospect, I got my laptop from the office and made myself comfortable on the sofa. Jack Frost stayed close by on the floor, and Snowflake cuddled next to my side. They were quite content having me home from work.

I went back over my notes in the blue notebook before getting online to check for messages on Strike a Match. There were the typical 'smiles' and 'likes' which I now saw as non committal ways of connecting — kind of like grabbing six flavors of ice cream in case you didn't like the first five. And who was I to judge someone for not wanting to commit? I didn't even date. I opened another message.

Good morning, fine specimen. I'm Doctor Kennedy, a professor of religion. Although I'm an atheist, I find your profile most intriguing. I have exquisite taste and would like you to accompany me for an evening of intellectual conversation and dining at a location of my choice. You may contact me and I will let you know when and where we will meet.

Oh, goody. We have So. Much. In. Common. I wonder what kind of mind altering gasses the clouds that circle around his head hold? There was no picture so the image I conjured up in my head made me laugh out loud. A skinny head with an upward pointed nose on an excessively long neck, and glassy eyes.

After an hour of reading and making notes, I rolled off the sofa to stretch out on the floor. It felt good to my back until Jack stood over me, his nose to my nose, wagging his tail. I wrapped my arms around his neck and laughed as he rolled onto his back for a tummy rub.

"Ah, Jack, you're a good boy. I guess I have been a little too busy lately, haven't I? Well, it looks like I'll be home for a while so we can catch up on your tummy rubs, okay?"

He wiggled around and jumped to his feet looking expectant. I rubbed his ears and said, "How about a treat?" He raced me to the kitchen and stood with his nose pointed toward the treat jar.

CHAPTER 8

a couple of days later as I sat on the sofa with my ankle up, I called Angie.

"Hi Mel! What's going on in Alaska?"

"Well, I have good news and bad news. The bad news is I broke my ankle. The good news is I have time to write and I decided this morning that this whole ankle thing might turn out to be a real blessing in disguise."

"Oh my word! First things first. How did you break your ankle? Have you had surgery?"

"It's a long story — at least the way I tell it." We both laughed. "I would rather tell you about it in person, but thank God, no surgery required. I'm bummed because I was planning a trip to Boise to check out the hospitals and meet with a contractor and now it's all on hold. It's so frustrating. I have all my lists in order and my timeline to move, settle in a new house, and start a new job. Now it's all messed up. If I can't meet with the contractor now, I'll be further down on his list and will have to rent something then move again when my house is finished. It's just not going according to my plan at all. Such a pain!"

"I'm so sorry, Mel. On the upside, once you move to Boise I can drive or fly out for a weekend now and then. And maybe I can be there when your house is done to help you move in. It'll be so great to be close enough to see each other again. I miss you."

"I miss you too and it will be fun. You could come out to get away from the big city and relax. We can go hiking, swimming, and take picnics with Jack Frost. You can help me pick out colors for my new home."

"You don't need my help with that. Your home is so warm and inviting. Oh Mel — why don't you come down while you're off with your ankle? Do you think you could travel?"

"I'm sure I can, but there aren't many ways out of Alaska so they kind of have us over a barrel. And I have money saved, but I want to keep some padding in my account because moving always costs more than you plan. Anyway, you have a great week."

"You too and heal quickly."

After talking to Angie, I emailed the contractor to let him know I wanted to meet with him but it would probably be late spring at the earliest. Then I contacted the hospitals in the Boise area to put out feelers and get a sense of each one so when I was able to go, they would hopefully remember me.

By the time I crossed those things off my list it was afternoon and my stomach growled. Jack looked at my stomach and growled, wagging his tail. "Okay, Jack, we will feed the monster and maybe share with you too." I went to the kitchen with a light heart while I hummed Kari Jobe's *I Am Not Alone.* As I sang the words, I realized that through all of the hard things that had happened the last few years, I had not been alone. Oh, I knew that in my head, but there were times that the heart ache and shame nearly overwhelmed me.

A new hope stirred in me, and even though I knew it came from God, the suddenness of it surprised me.

The next few days I referred to my red notebook numerous times trying to figure out the logistics of a move of twenty-six hundred miles by myself. *God, please help me make wise decisions in this time of transition. I'm ready to move on and begin anew, but I need you to lead me.*

One morning as I went through the house, I wondered how I would pull this move off. All the lovely furniture I had purchased over the years and things that had been gifted to me — so many nice things. I sensed the Holy Spirit asking me, *Could you give all this up?*

I surveyed the beautiful furnishings, lush plants, crystal vases, the fine china. *Wow. I never thought of that, Lord. That would simplify everything about the move. Here I've been stressing about how to take it all with me. If I were to give it up, I could load Jack and Snowflake into the car with the things we need and truly start over. No worries about how to transport or move it all into my new home. That's a great idea. Yes! I could give it all up, Lord.*

The rest of the day I felt incredibly light — as though a huge weight had lifted from my shoulders. I hummed praise songs as I tore pages from the red notebook that pertained to moving companies and prices of rental trucks. I laughed while I tore those pages into small pieces and dropped them into the trash.

Nicole turned from the medicine cabinet and looked at me. "What do you mean you're getting rid of everything? Mel, what kind of pain meds have you been taking? Have you really thought about this?"

I laughed at her reaction and figured it might be similar to my own if the shoe were on the other foot. Or the walking boot for that matter. "I know it sounds radical, but at the same time it makes perfect sense."

"What are you doing with yourself while you're off work? Are you okay?"

"I'm of sound mind and mostly of body." I grinned. "Yes, I'm fine. I've been making lists for the move and doing as much as I can on that topic and working on my book too. I have to admit I'm getting antsy. I needed some groceries and after going to the store, I wasn't quite ready to go home so thought I'd check in here and see how everyone is doing."

Dr. Fletcher came from a patient room. "Amelia, what a nice surprise. We miss you around here."

"Thank you, I miss you guys too. But I'm trying to use my unexpected time off productively. Making lists, working on my book, spending time with my critters." I looked back to Nicole. "I spoke with my friend in Seattle yesterday and she invited me to come down for a few days to break up the monotony."

"Oh that would be nice for you. Are you going?"

"No, I had planned to make a trip to Idaho and meet with the HR departments and a contractor about a house but it will have to wait. I'm not happy about the delay. I just want order in my life. I meticulously make plans and try to list everything so all goes accordingly. This little accident was not on my list." I sighed. "Anyway, I don't really have fun travel funds right now. I had budgeted for the trip to find work and housing as part of moving expenses. Funny, when I broke my ankle I was actually on my way here to see about getting a few days off to take that trip. I have an emergency fund, but a trip to see a friend is not an emergency." I laughed.

"Amelia, come sit down a minute. Give your ankle a rest," Dr. Fletcher ordered.

I shrugged at Nicole. "Bossy, isn't he?" We both laughed.

Setting my crutches aside, I sat down in the chair next to Dr. Fletcher at his work station. "What's up, Doc?"

He looked down at his computer screen as he spoke. "You know, there's great skiing in Vancouver B.C. I've been thinking about going to Whistler Blackcomb for a long weekend. Maybe spend four days there. I'd fly into Seattle and rent a car."

"That sounds like fun for a skier. Have you skied there before?"

"I have. Look, I have a companion fare that's going to expire. Why don't you come with me?"

"What? Uh, what do you mean?"

He looked over at me and laughed. "Your face is as red as a beet. You wear red well. What I mean is why don't you use my companion fare and go see your friend? The fare requires that the companion fly on the same flights so you could fly down with me, I can take you to your friend's house, and then drive to B.C. I can pick you up on the way back if you like, and we'll fly home together."

"Oh, no, I couldn't accept that."

He looked back at his computer screen. "Why not? If I don't use it this month it will go to waste and that would be a shame — especially when I have a friend who could use a little break. But I need to know right away so I can make the reservations." He looked over at me and raised an eyebrow.

"I want to go by the coffee stand. Can I get back to you later? This evening maybe?"

He pulled a sticky note off a pad and jotted something down before handing it to me. "This is my cell number. Just give me a call and a yea or nay. I'll be home this evening."

I took the note and stuck it in my pocket, then looked around to see if anyone was watching us. Fortunately everyone seemed to be minding their own business — for a change. "Thank you for the offer either way. It was really generous of you."

"Not at all. Like I said, it will go to waste if it's not used this month."

Instead of getting coffee that I would have to drink in the lobby as I couldn't carry it using two crutches, I decided to go home. As I drove, Mitch's offer ran through my head. *Lord, what should I do? He seemed sincere that he just wanted to share the fare with me. I need advice. Please help me know what to do.*

It was almost ten thirty when I got my groceries put away. I went to my office to try to spend some time working on the book. I pulled up Strike a Match and had a message from a guy named Lyle.

Hey, lovely lady. I'm a widowed rancher. I have five kids. The twins are eight-year-old boys, my daughters are eleven and thirteen-years-old, and my oldest son is fifteen-years-old. We have cattle and horses and a few sheep. I'm looking for a woman who can feed a hungry crew and help me raise my kids. Someone who will keep me company when they're all grown. I don't have time to go to church, but I find God out on the range. Check out my profile and then let me know when you're available and I'll bring you out to meet the family.

There's an honest man. No doubt not afraid of work. And it sounds like his hands are full. I hope he finds what he's looking for. I pasted my standard reply and hit send.

Jack came into my office and set his chin on my leg. I looked down at his hopeful eyes and he wagged his tail.

"What's up, Jack?" His tail wagged faster.

"Maybe you sense that I'm getting hungry and you want me to make food to share?"

He barked. "Inside voice, Jack." He barked softer. "Good boy. Let's go find some food."

I looked in the fridge at the groceries I'd just purchased,

but grabbed some cheese and an apple. Even though I'd gotten out of the house for a little bit, I still felt antsy. I struggled with the way my little accident had messed up all my plans. I've always liked order, but after Jeff died, it wasn't just something I wanted, it was something I needed. A sense of control.

I went to the office and got my blue notebook. I flipped the pages and studied my notes, but found myself reading the same paragraphs over and over. I went to the kitchen and made my blended coffee, but after a couple of sips I dumped it in the sink. *What is wrong with me?* I felt like I was sparring in a match with an unseen opponent. Everything I tried to do, I either couldn't complete or had to redo. Finally, I went to the kitchen and pulled out ingredients to make cookies. Surely I could do that. When I pulled the third tray from the oven my phone rang and I jumped and burned my arm. I held the phone with one hand while running cold water over my other arm. "Hello?"

"Hey, Mel," Angie said in a bright voice.

"Oh hi, Ang."

"Did I call at a bad time? You don't sound like yourself."

"No, I just burned my arm and I feel like I've managed to mess up everything I've set my hand to today."

"That doesn't sound like you," her voice resonated with concern.

"It's not like me. A week ago I was high on life even with a broken ankle, seeing the bright side of things and all the possibilities — and now I feel like I got on the horse, and the saddle slid under his belly leaving me hanging upside down."

"Mel, you are the most positive person I know, but we all have low days. Even you. You wear that eternal smile, but you've had some hard knocks too. Just because you don't show the scars doesn't mean there aren't any. Cut yourself some slack. Do you need to talk?"

"Actually I think I need to listen. I've been making these plans, praying all along and they had gone without a hitch until the accident, but it's almost like I'm missing something. I think I need to do a fast and just listen. I don't want to make another drastic mistake and see more lives ruined."

"Okay, stop. When you got married you trusted Jeff and why wouldn't you? Just because he wasn't who he claimed or pretended to be doesn't make it your fault. Don't take blame that isn't yours. You answer to God for your sins and let Jeff answer to God for his. Jesus came to carry all that, not Mel."

"Thank you. I know you're right. Once in a while I just slip back on that path. So, how are you doing? Anything exciting going on in your life?"

"Not really. I just miss you. I wish you could have come down, but you will eventually. I miss our talks and our laughs."

"I miss you too, Ang. Oh, you won't believe what happened today."

"What? Tell me."

"I had to get out of the house and went by work. I was talking to Nicole about your invite to come when Dr. Fletcher called me over to his desk. He said he wanted to go skiing in B.C. and invited me to come."

She squealed. "What? Are you kidding me? With a broken ankle? What did you say?"

"He explained that he had a companion fare that expires this month and asked if I wanted to fly down with him to come see you while he goes skiing."

"Oh wow, that would be amazing. I want to see you so bad When are you coming?"

"Seriously? You think I should accept his offer?"

"Why wouldn't you? You miss me, don't you?" She giggled.

"That's a silly question. I'm supposed to call him this

evening to let him know because he said it's about to expire. Do you really think I should tell him yes?"

"Of course I do. Just tell me when you'll be here and I'll make arrangements to pick you up."

"Wow. I guess I could tell him okay — as long as he lets me pay the companion fee at least. I really don't have the budget to buy a ticket, but I can pay that much. He said he thought he'd ski for four days."

"Then it's settled. Get back to me with the details. I can't wait to see you."

"Okay, I'll call him. I'm nervous about this, but I gotta admit I'm so excited to spend a few days with you."

"Me too. And since you're on crutches, maybe I can keep up with you." She snorted.

"Oh, funny girl. I love you and I'll text you with info."

I decided I was hungry enough to eat a bite, so went to the kitchen with Jack at my heels. I took a cookie from the jar and broke it in half to share with Jack. "Argh. I was starting a fast, Jack. Here, you can have my half too." He gently took it from my hand.

After debating with myself for a few minutes, I picked up my phone and put Mitch's number in my contacts before dialing him.

"Hello?"

My hands felt damp. "Dr. — Mitch, this is Mel." I cleared my throat.

"Amelia. I'm so glad you called. So have you made a decision?"

"Yes. I mean yes I will go, but I want to pay you for the companion fee."

"That's not necessary."

"It is to me. I really appreciate your generous offer, but let me cover that. Okay?

"Whatever."

I could hear the smile in the way he said the overused word. "Thank you."

"Great. I'll book our reservations. It will be pleasant to have you as a travel companion."

"Thank you, good night Mitch."

"Good night, Amelia."

I sat on the floor in front of the fire a while with Jack's chin on my leg and Snowball in my lap. I pet one with each hand and enjoyed the comfort of their company and loyalty. "You guys are great, you know? We make a good team." *Thank you, God for bringing these two into my life.* And I believed He truly did. Snowball had been rescued by a paramedic friend who couldn't take her home due to his daughter's allergies. The kitten was barely old enough to be weaned when Chris had called to ask if I'd take her. Jack Frost had shown up on my doorstep when I had friends over for a bar-b-cue the next summer. I'd tried to find his owner — surely someone missed such a nice young dog, but no one claimed him. That was six years ago. Now we were simply a little family. They didn't ask questions I couldn't or didn't want to answer. Unconditional love.

That night I had difficulty going to sleep. Whether it was excitement about the upcoming trip or something else I wasn't sure, but I tossed and turned until after one o'clock. Finally I got up and went down the hall to the kitchen. The critters were sweetly lying together in front of the fire. My heart melted. I went to the fridge to grab some water and stopped to watch Jack and Snowball sleep peacefully. That's when I heard it. *Could you give them up?*

"What? God?" I whispered. "You wouldn't ask me to do that. Why would you? You're the one who brought them into my life in the first place? NO."

The next morning I needed to go to town to take care of business, including stopping by to ask Margie if she could stay with the critters while I was in Seattle. Ellen waved me over.

"You can't stay away from here, can you? I know the feeling." She laughed.

"Yep, gotta love this place. Well, I do love my coworkers." I smiled.

She finished charting on the computer and stood up. "How are your plans going for the big move?"

"Delayed. I was going to fly down to meet with a contractor and meet with a couple HR department heads — the day you took care of my ankle I was setting up my trip."

"Oh that's frustrating. I'm sorry. A break — sorry for the choice of word — an escape to somewhere a little warmer would be nice about now. Winter is beautiful but so long."

"I agree. That's one of the big reasons I'm making the move."

"What move?" Dr. Martinez came from behind me. "You're serious about moving? What about Mitch?"

My face reddened. "What about Dr. Fletcher?"

Dr. Martinez grinned. "Oh you know how rumors are around this place? It's like a little town where everyone knows everyone else's business."

I smiled. "Or at least likes to think they do, right?" Ellen laughed and Doc went to his computer station shaking his head.

"There's Margie now, I'm going to catch her before anyone else catches me. Have a great day, Ellen."

"You too, Mel. I miss working with you." She leaned in and gave me a quick hug.

Margie put her purse in her desk drawer, locked it and placed the key around her wrist. "How long will you be gone?"

"Six days, and if you can't do it, don't worry about it, Margie. I can hire one of the college kids from church."

"I adore your house, and Jack and Snowball are great. No, don't call someone else. I would love to stay there for you. I felt so much peace in your house and usually I only feel turmoil. Thank you for asking me."

"Margie, the peace is God, you know?"

"I'm not biting on that one, but I do know the peace was real. I experienced it at Christmas. When can I come out?"

"I'm leaving early in the morning, so you come after work the night before if you'd like. With you there for the evening the critters might not get so upset about me leaving."

"Sounds good. I'll come right after work. You going to make me dinner?" She batted her eyes.

I laughed. "I will make you dinner and the fridge will be stocked." Holding my crutches in one hand, I gave her a quick one armed hug and walked to the exit. I put the ice grips down on my crutches and walked gingerly to my car.

A couple of evenings later I had my leg up on the sofa and my laptop in my lap. Jack was on the floor at my side and Snowball was smooshed up against my side purring. I'd been working on my book and needed a break so pulled up Strike a Match. A message from Chuck read, "Hello angle." *He must be an engineer — I've been wrongly called an angel but an angle? That's a new one.* "I have been searching for so long and I'm sure you are the answer to my prayers. Please write me back right away."

Ah poor Chuck, if I was nice I'd send him a Pi. I giggled at my pun. Snowball stretched and flexed her claws in my thigh.

"Okay, Snowball! I know it was a bad pun but you don't have to get catty about it." I laughed and picked her up to place a kiss on her soft ear. She opened one eye then closed it and purred contentedly.

CHAPTER 9

*M*argie arrived at my house after work late Wednesday afternoon. "Oh man, it smells good in here." She hung her coat on the rack and scooped Snowball into her arms. Jack greeted her then came back to supervise me in the kitchen.

"I made a roast and veggies — there's enough here for you to have plenty of leftovers. And I left my recipe on the fridge for vegetable soup that you can make with the left over roast if you'd like. Or you could make pot pie or even enchiladas." I whisked the gravy.

"I'm not a cook, Mel. I will eat whatever you make but then I'll just eat left overs."

"It's not rocket science, Margie." I set a platter on the table and handed her the gravy bowl.

"Maybe not to you." She wrinkled her nose at me reminding me of a little kid.

"Do you want water or juice?"

"Juice. I don't like water."

I smiled to myself as I poured juice into a glass. Yep, just like a little kid.

We finished dinner and I showed her labeled containers in the freezer and fridge. "Margie, help yourself to whatever sounds good. I really appreciate you taking care of things while I'm away."

"I'm the one who benefits most. So would you like me to drive you to the airport tomorrow?"

I hung the kitchen towel on the hook. "No, but thank you. I appreciate you taking care of things here. That's enough to ask of you."

"But I don't mind taking you and I can pick you up in a warm car when you get back. Really, I want to take you."

This was going to be tricky. "Okay, so Margie — I already have a ride, but thank you."

"Okay."

After an early dinner I put on my pajamas while Margie hung out with the critters.

Not being a night person, I sat on the sofa yawning while Margie watched a movie. When I finally went to bed, I couldn't sleep. The next morning I packed my makeup after I finished my sparse makeup routine.

I placed it in my carry-on and then set it by the door with my coat. I noted the time and watched for Mitch to come up the driveway. I saw his headlights and I stood and crossed the room to get my coat. I was hoping I could get outside, but Mitch made it to the door and rang the bell. The light from the living room illuminated the porch where he was standing.

"Oh momma mia!" Margie covered her mouth with her hand. "Is that — that *is* Dr. Fletcher."

I knew this would be awkward. I should have let her drop me off at the airport and she wouldn't have seen him. "Yes, it is." I opened the door. "Thank you for taking me, Dr. Fletcher. I hope it wasn't out of your way."

His eyes twinkled. "No, you were on my way," he played

along. "And I'm happy to take you to the airport." He glanced at my carry-on. "Is that your only bag?"

"Yes, and we should go as I don't want to take up all your time." I turned to Margie who sat there with her mouth gaping. "Margie, you have my number if you need anything at all. Thank you so much for taking care of things for me."

"I think I have your number. Yes, I do think I have your number," she grinned widely and nodded.

Mitch lifted my bag and took my arm with his other hand. He opened the car door for me then placed my bag in the back seat. He got in the car and laughed. "You were in a hurry to get out of there."

"Well, having you show up at my door to take me to the airport appears like more that it is to some people. If you know what I mean."

He laughed again. "And you work so hard to avoid those appearances."

"Yes, I do. I don't want people to get the wrong impression. Oh, I have something for you." I pulled the cash from my purse to cover the companion fare.

"Amelia, you really don't need to do that."

"But—"

"Then just hang onto it until we get to the airport."

Mitch dropped me at the terminal then went to park the car. I made my way to the gate to wait for him. He arrived carrying our luggage. He sat down and I remained standing a few feet away so if we were recognized people wouldn't assume we were together. Several people said hello to him. When the agent called for early boarding and first class, Mitch signaled me with a nod. I supposed I should board early with my crutches so I wouldn't hold up the line.

He stood and came up beside me, showing the tickets on his phone to the boarding agent. She said, "Welcome aboard Mr. and Mrs. Fletcher. Have a nice flight."

My face felt hot, but Mitch just said, "Thank you, I think we will." He carried both of our carry-ons and motioned for me to go ahead of him. When we got inside the aircraft, a flight attendant greeted us and Mitch stopped me. "These are our seats, Amelia." He pointed to row one, seats A, and B in first class.

"Seriously? But —"

"The companion fare is the same, why wouldn't I fly you first class?" He waited for me to sit by the window then handed my crutches to the flight attendant.

I felt a little like an imposture. "Oh, here is the money I owe you." I reached in my pocket and held the money out to him. He wrapped his hand over mine and closed my fingers.

"I don't want this to be an obligation. I wanted to come ski, I like to fly first class and I had a companion fare to use. Please accept it."

What could I say? "Thank you, Mitch. I guess we are going to be at a stand off if one of us doesn't give in, aren't we?"

He grinned. "Now you're getting it, Amelia."

The flight attendant took drink orders while other passengers were boarding.

"Dr. Fletcher! Going on another ski trip?"

I looked up at the familiar voice to see Skip, from the lab. *Oh no — the grapevine will be bearing fruit by morning.*

Mitch said, "Yes, Skip. Where are you off to?"

"I'm just meeting up with some buddies in Seattle for a few days. Quality guy time, you know?" He looked at me. "So Mel, I know people have a golf handicap, but skiing? Really?"

I felt agitated. "Nah, actually I thought I'd try snowboarding. The crutches will help me push off to gain speed."

The flight attendant urged Skip to move to his seat and I wanted to hug her.

Mitch leaned towards me and grinned. "You avoided his quest for information very nicely."

I shrugged. "He was on a fishing expedition and I imagine there will be quite a fish story going around by the time we get back."

Mitch put his head back and laughed. "You have a great sense of humor, Mel."

The flight attendant was attentive to the first class customers, bringing us beverages, food, and making sure we were comfortable. Mitch and I chatted about work, kids and our separate plans for the long weekend. When the captain came on the intercom to say that we were preparing to land, it almost seemed too soon. I don't know why it surprised me that we were so comfortable together since we'd worked together well for several years. But I'd always kept my personal and professional life as separate as possible.

Mitch picked up the rental car and had me put Angie's address in his phone for directions. When we arrived at her apartment, I texted her we had arrived. She came out and hugged me and I introduced her to Mitch. He insisted on taking my carry-on to her door. "Amelia, are you going to be okay on the stairs," he asked.

"Of course. I have stairs at home and I've done fine on them. Except the time I forgot to put the ice grip up on my crutch and stuck it in my foot." I bugged my eyes.

Mitch winked and said, "Maybe it's a good thing you don't ski."

"Yeah, just think of the damage I could do with ski poles."

He and Angie both nodded and laughed.

"Okay, you ladies have fun. I'm going to hit the road so I can hit the slopes. Amelia I will see you Tuesday morning."

Angie said, "Oh I could take her to the airport."

"I'm going to be going there anyway so it's no problem." He looked at me. "It's not, is it?"

"No, that's great, thank you. I really appreciate everything, Mitch. I owe you."

Angie's apartment was small but well appointed. Her living room window faced the garden area in the back of the building. "What a nice view to have."

Angie laughed. "You are being nice now. I've been to your house and know you have a view of the Brooks range from your living room window. This can't touch looking out and seeing Denali with her head in the clouds."

"You're right, but now you're in Seattle, and considering you live in an apartment, this is a nice view. It looks well kept. I think you found yourself a nice place."

"I looked at a lot of places and the rents are exorbitant, so I am blessed to have found this one. Actually a co-worker lived here and she got married right when I started working, so I was able to just take over her lease. Timing was everything."

Angie took my bag to the guest room and I followed her. "Sorry this is so sparse. The only room I've done much with is the living room. I still have some unpacked boxes in the closet."

I sat on the edge of the bed. "Well, this feels comfy and there are curtains for privacy and a door to get out — or get in. What else do I really need?" I fell back on the bed and sighed. "I can't believe I'm actually here and we get four whole days together. Wait, did you say unpacked boxes? You know if you haven't needed anything out of them by now, you probably don't need it at all."

She laughed. "You leave my unpacked boxes alone! I'm so happy you're here. And Mitch — what's going on there? He's quite good looking. And he seems so nice." She sat down on the edge of the bed.

"Nothing is going on. We're just friends. I have been running into him a lot the last few months though. Which is kinda weird since we've worked together for a while and I never used to see him around town. Then before Christmas it seemed I'd turn around and there he was. At *The Book and Bean*, the ballet — kinda odd now that I think about it."

"Maybe he ran into you accidentally on purpose?"

"Of course not. Hey, thank you for taking the afternoon off to spend it with me."

"It worked out well because I do have vacation time and you're here over the weekend so I only had to take two days. There's a place we're going for brunch on Saturday called the Silver Porche. I haven't been, but I've heard rave reviews, and if you don't have reservations you could wait in line for a long time. I made reservations." She blew on her fist and pretended to shine it on her shoulder.

"Wow, sounds like it must be good if it's that popular. How fun! And don't worry that I might slow us down with my crutches. I can actually run with them. Although it works better if I have shoes on and the ice grip isn't down." We laughed.

"You poor thing, that had to hurt."

"Oh Ang, I was baking cookies the day you called me — the day I burnt my hand — and I turned around fast in the kitchen and nearly broke the glass on the oven door with my crutch. I don't move slow enough for these things. But you'll be safe from potential muggers with me because I'm lethal with them." I reached over to grab a crutch and jabbed it in the air.

She laughed. "I miss hanging out with you and laughing together. Everything seems more tolerable with you."

"I feel the same way. We've had some good laughs — and we've shared a few tears too. We've been blessed with a special friendship and I thank God for that. And now we have time to catch up. We could even get rid of some unpacked boxes." I giggled.

"Hey, you leave my boxes alone."

"So where are those boxes hiding?"

She grabbed a throw pillow and tossed it at me. "There's only a couple. I actually listened to you and got rid of some stuff. You were right. I wasn't using what was in them and realized I didn't have any need for the stuff now. It felt kinda good to donate those things."

I stood up and looked out the window. "I forget how green it is in other parts of the country this time of year. It's so pretty. I can't wait to live where spring is a season. At home we have break-up, summer, maybe fall, and winter — no spring. Look at all the flowers." I opened the window and took a deep breath.

We spent the first day catching up and enjoying being together to talk about whatever came to mind — like we did when we lived closer. Angie had all the ingredients for strawberry spinach salad and roasted chicken breasts. She said, "Now if we only had some fresh bread to go with this. Nice, warm, fresh bread." She grinned at me.

"Do you have yeast, flour, salt?"

"You betcha! Will you really make us some?"

"How about braided bread sticks brushed with garlic and kosher salt?"

"Yes! I'll get the ingredients out."

"Good, the dough will have time to rise and we can have them warm from the oven with our meal. You can help me do the braids," I said.

Within an hour the braided sticks were placed in a warm oven to rise. She'd gotten quick rise yeast which was perfect as we only had to do one rise. Angie said, "Since it's fairly nice out, I thought we'd eat on the balcony so you can enjoy the flowers."

The heady smell of freshly baked bread permeated the

small apartment when we filled our plates and went out on the balcony. Angie dropped slices of lemon in our water.

I surveyed the little garden from the balcony as we sat down at the table. "This is perfect, Ang. Thank you for inviting me down. It's been kind of chaotic the last few months. With work, trying to plan my move and then breaking my ankle — which put all my plans on the back burner."

She nodded. "I know that's had to be difficult for you. You've always been such a planner and organizer. It must be like having a big wind come in and blow everything off of your desk."

"Yes, that's exactly how it feels. Like all of my plans being blown out of my hands. Don't you wish sometimes that you could see what God's plans are? I mean like when you get one of those tickets that you have to scratch off to find out how much your discount will be? Sometimes you toss them because they aren't worth the trouble. Hmmm."

"Hmmm what?" She took a bite of bread. "This is so yummy."

"Everything on my plate is yummy. The 'hmmm' was a thought I had. What if you could do the scratch off to see His plan and didn't think it looked good so you tossed it? Like you get two percent off your next purchase — big deal. But if you had actually accepted it you would have discovered that everything in the store was ninety percent off just for you — on top of the two percent. It would have been worth investigating what originally seemed of little value."

"Interesting thought, Mel. So maybe it's good we can't see His plan, because we might think we know better, when we're only seeing the surface. You know, even when I got this job I only saw a little. I worried that I'd have a hard time finding a decent apartment and everything. But the timing of the job and the apartment coming open, made it clear that

He was watching out for me. I had looked at places further away from work and not as nice, but they cost just as much. And I have good neighbors here."

"Yeah, why are we so prone to worry?" I took a bite of strawberry.

"Because we're women? I don't know."

That evening we put on our pajamas, made popcorn and watched an old comedy — and laughed until we cried.

On Friday we mostly hung out around Angie's apartment aside from a little run to a natural foods market. She let me browse and ooh and ahh to my hearts content. I picked up a few things to take home.

Since you could never predict the traffic, we left early Saturday morning to arrive on time for our reservation at the Silver Porche.

Angie was a good driver — attentive — so we talked while she drove, but she would go quiet when the traffic got crazy — which in my mind was all the time. When we arrived at our destination, she spotted a parking spot and smoothly parallel parked.

The Silver Porche had a line of waiting customers more than a block long. Angie led the way around them and opened the door. She gave her name at the hostess desk where a young woman dressed in a crisp white shirt and black pants checked a list before asking us to follow her. We walked past a case displaying baked goods and my mouth salivated. Colorful macarons, beautiful cakes, and tasty looking breads. The rich aroma of coffee heightened my senses. This was going to be a treat.

We were seated at a small round table with chairs that looked like luxury auto seats. The hostess handed us menus and as she walked away a young man approached our table and set down glasses of ice water, a small plate with sliced lemon and white linen napkins. "Good morning, ladies, I'm Chad and I'll be your server today."

Our order came sooner than I expected since the place was packed, and the meal was wonderful. "Oh, thank you for bringing me here. My croissant was almost too cute to eat, but I'm glad I did. I've never seen a fish shaped croissant before. And the salmon and cream cheese filling in the light pastry — perfect. And you can't get fresh fruit like this in Alaska this time of year. Yum."

Angie laughed. "If I didn't have my own brunch I'd be coveting yours, Mel. It is good, isn't it? I haven't been here before but some friends at work told me I should try it. I'm glad they told me to make reservations. And I'm so happy we got to try it together." She picked up her coffee cup and held it out to me. "Here's to you moving much closer so we can have these fun outings more often."

I clicked my cup to hers. "Hear. Hear. I second that."

When Chad brought the check, I grabbed it. Angie said, "Mel, I was taking you out for brunch."

"You did and I appreciate it. I don't want to feel like a free-loader. Mitch wouldn't take my money for the companion fare and we flew first class. He said he wanted me to be comfortable. Anyway, I have the money I was trying to give to him."

"That was very considerate of him. Nice looking, considerate, polite — does he have a sense of humor?"

"Yes, he does. You almost have to if you work in an ER — unless you are unbearable to work with." I laughed. "Hey, I already introduced you to him. Now you're on your own."

"Yes, you did, but I think the commute would make getting acquainted challenging." She twisted her hair on her finger and grinned. "So I was thinking we'd go to Pike's Market. Are you up for that?"

"Of course I am. I haven't been there in years. I bet it will be crowded today being Saturday. But we aren't in a hurry. And I'm with my best friend."

Angie drove around a while trying to find a parking spot. "Is this going to be too far?"

"I get around fine. I wouldn't use the crutches at all now but I want my ankle to heal properly so I don't have problems later. I can do this, girl."

We spent the afternoon strolling the market place, checking out shops, looking at the vender's offerings and watching other people. An adorable young man was selling fish and had obviously worked on his sales routine. Angie and I laughed in delight as we watched him appeal to potential customers. I decided to support him and indulge our taste buds and bought some fresh halibut to grill while I was in town.

Sunday morning Angie and I woke early so we lounged around her apartment drinking coffee and eating fruit. After a couple of hours she asked, "So are you up for going to church with me?"

"Absolutely, I'll get a quick shower and get dressed. Casual or what?"

"They'll take you as you are."

"Well, I'll still take a shower and get dressed in something besides my pajamas. Or is the service held at Walmart?" We both laughed.

I was drawn in by the worship music and lifted my hands in praise to my Savior. After the music time, the pastor read the passage in Mark 6:45-52, where Jesus sent his disciples out in a boat while he went up on a mountainside to pray. A storm gathered, and Jesus saw the disciples struggling in the boat against the strong winds, so he walked across the top of the water toward them. When the disciples saw Jesus walking on water, they thought he was a ghost and they were terrified. Jesus reassured them and told them not to be afraid because it was him, and then he got into the boat with them and the stormy winds died down.

I'd felt like I'd been in a storm for a while when Jeff died and now my plans were being tossed by 'choppy waters', but I had assurance yet again that I was not alone. God knew His plans for me even if I didn't. I'd take the two percent scratch off bonus and trust Him.

Tears of relief spilled down my cheeks. I felt Angie take my hand. I squeezed her hand. *Thank you, Father that you have plans and you won't leave me alone in a storm of uncertainty. Help me to trust you more.*

We got back to the apartment and made lunch together. We talked about the message that morning and what it meant to each of us. We agreed that we both battled fear at times and how that could distract us. I told Angie, "When I'm worrying about the waves, my eyes are on the water instead of on the One who's there to keep me from drowning. I'm my own worst enemy sometimes. I want to be in control, but when the elements around me toss the boat, there has to be someone bigger who can control the boat."

Angie led the way and carried our lunch plates to the balcony. "Exactly — I know I have plenty to meditate on this week. I'm glad you were there this morning. I love that we can process and discuss it together."

"It does help to have someone to bounce our thoughts off of. I'm glad I was there, too. Good food for thought."

CHAPTER 10

*M*onday morning, Angie and I went out for coffee and a bagel. We didn't have an agenda for the last day of our visit, aside from enjoying each other's company. When we got back to her apartment, we ran into Mr. Stroud, one of her neighbors.

"Good morning, ladies. How are you on this beautiful Seattle morning?"

Angie said, "Hi, Mr. Stroud. We went out to get a cup of coffee. How are you doing?"

"Oh, I'm fine. Can't complain." He smiled, but I thought his eyes looked sad.

When we got into her apartment, I asked about him.

"He's the sweetest. His wife died a few years ago after fifty-two years of marriage. I think he gets pretty lonely sometimes, but he is such a sweet neighbor to everyone."

"That's sad. It would be so hard to lose someone you have spent your life with. Does he have family around?"

"He has a son in Olympia. He goes there at least twice a year — Christmas and in the summer for a few days."

Angie brought out the two boxes she hadn't unpacked and set them on her living room floor. "Okay, let's do it."

"What? You're going to surrender the last of your unpacked boxes?" I lifted my eyebrows in mock surprise.

"Why not? You can witness it. In fact you can help me. I only have these two because I thought the stuff would be harder to deal with due to sentimental value."

"It's okay to be sentimental, Angie. It's okay to keep things that mean a lot to you."

"But you told me how God had asked you if you could give everything up."

"He did, I think it's because hanging onto everything would have made my move much more difficult."

"People move everyday and take their things with them. Why would He ask you to give your stuff up?"

"I don't know. He asked me if I *could*. It wasn't like He gave me a command written on a stone tablet." I laughed.

Angie laughed. "Well, I'm ready to go through these boxes. Are you going to help me?"

I sat on the floor beside her. "Let's do this."

A while later she had two piles. One pile of things to keep and one pile to recycle. I suggested she get a storage container that would fit on her closet shelf and recycle the cardboard box too. She said, "I agree. That will look nicer and be more like these are things I value. Good idea." She put the recycle pile into the boxes and took them downstairs to the recycle bin. While she did that, I made a neat pile of what remained and slipped it into a bag to keep it together until she got a container for it. When she came back to the apartment, she stopped in the doorway. "Mel, would you mind if we invited Mr. Stroud to join us for lunch?"

"That's a great idea, of course I don't mind."

"I wanted to invite him before but I never did because I didn't want people to gossip."

"I understand. Why don't you go invite him?

Later the three of us sat at Angie's small dining table enjoying a tasty lunch of grilled halibut and fresh vegetables. Mr. Stroud regaled us with stories of his life. When he spoke of his wife, it was if she was in the room with him — the memory of her still so strong in his mind. But rather than seeming sad, he became animated. I deduced that thinking of her brought him joy. Eventually he turned to me and said, "Amelia, do you have someone special in your life?"

"No, Mr. Stroud, my husband died."

He reached over and put his hand over mine. "I do understand the deep loss." He squeezed my hand and patted it before removing his.

I nodded. I couldn't tell him that I didn't miss the man my husband had become. I stood up and gathered our dishes. Angie slid back from the table. "Mel, let me do that."

"Angie I can get around fine in your little kitchen without crutches. I'm not an invalid."

"I know, but please sit here with our guest and I'll get dessert."

I sat back down. "Okay." I looked across at Mr. Stroud. "I guess we get to be waited on hand and foot today. Aren't we special?"

"Yes, I guess we are indeed." He laughed then put his open hand on his chest.

I noticed his expression change. "Mr. Stroud? Are you all right? Are you having chest pains?"

"No, I'm fine, young lady. I've just been having these bouts lately. Probably gallbladder. I had problems with that before."

"Do you feel short of breath? Nauseous? Pain in your jaw or radiating to your back or neck?"

He tried to smile as he nodded. "Yes."

"I suggest we call 911 and have an ambulance come. Are you okay with that?"

Angie turned to me, her eyes wide and her brows furrowed. "Mr. Stroud?"

"I hate to be a bother."

Angie said, "You are certainly not a bother. Mel's an ER nurse. If she thinks you need to go to the hospital, I hope you will agree to go."

He grimaced and his shoulders moved forward. "Ang, call 911," I said.

"Mr. Stroud, let's get you comfortable until the ambulance arrives." I unbuttoned his top shirt button. While Angie was on the phone, I assisted him to the sofa where he could recline. I lifted his feet up on the sofa and asked, "Do you take any medications?"

"No."

"Are you allergic to aspirin?" I unbuttoned the first couple of buttons on his shirt.

He shook his head. "No."

"Ang, do you have any aspirin?"

She shook her head then darted out the door. I heard quick knocking and then voices in the hall. Shortly she came back followed by an older woman who held out an aspirin bottle. I took it, shook out an aspirin and handed the bottle back. I asked Ang to bring him a sip of water and then I helped Mr. Stroud take the aspirin. Soon I heard the comforting sound of a siren in the not too far distance.

The older woman still clutched the aspirin bottle in her hand as she left the apartment to go downstairs to wait for the paramedics and direct them to Angie's apartment.

The paramedics arrived and I gave them a quick report of what had transpired, then let them take over and do their job. Mr. Stroud looked overwhelmed. Angie said, "Mel, what can we do? I don't want him to be alone."

I asked the paramedic, "What hospital are you taking him to?"

"Harborview. You can meet us there." They strapped Mr. Stroud on the gurney and headed out the door.

"Ang, are you okay? Do you want to go to the hospital?"

"I do, but it's your last day here."

"For crying out loud, you know that loving your neighbor is a commandment, whereas hanging out with your friend is not." I grinned. "Are you okay to drive?"

"Yes," She nodded. "Yes, I can drive. Will you come with me?"

"Try to make me stay here," I smiled. "And I'm glad you're able to drive because I don't know how to drive a stick shift."

"Seriously? I never knew that about you."

"A girl's gotta have a few secrets. I'll grab some water for us. Do you need anything else?"

"No." We started out the door and she stopped before I could pull the door shut behind me. "Well, maybe car keys would be helpful." She stepped back in and grabbed them from the stand and looked at me sheepishly. "Yes, I really can drive. I'm okay."

I smiled. "I didn't say anything." We laughed as we went down the stairs to her car.

At the hospital we were directed to a waiting room and were told that someone would come get us when they were ready. Angie looked at me.

"It's okay. Standard procedure. They need to give him a semblance of privacy while they move him onto a hospital gurney, dress him in a designer hospital gown, get the blood pressure and oxygen monitors on him, get an IV started. All that fun stuff we ER people live for."

She smiled. "Okay." She looked around the waiting room. There were some children playing with toys in the corner and a couple of older men talking rather loudly. "Let's sit near the door in case the nurse comes so we will hear them call us."

I handed Ang a bottle of water I'd brought along. "Here, stay hydrated."

"Yes, ma'am." She grinned and took the bottle.

I surveyed the people in the waiting room. I'd seen many families and friends waiting to find out about loved ones. I'd been on that end of the scenario more than once myself and understood the stress they experienced. Waiting was the most difficult part. I wondered what had brought these individuals to the ER on a Monday afternoon in Seattle. I was lost in my thoughts when the ER door opened but no one called Angie.

I heard two male voices talking. They stopped right beside us. I could see the doctor but couldn't read his name tag without my glasses. The paramedic he spoke to wore a baseball cap and had his back to us. I turned my attention back to the people waiting so they wouldn't feel as though I were eavesdropping.

The doctor spoke. "The patients are blessed to have you bring them in. And these new medics are blessed to have you back here to train them."

"I'm just doing my job."

"Praying over them isn't your job. You're a good man."

"God is good, not me. And praying for people is my job. Love your neighbor, right?"

I couldn't explain, but I sensed something familiar. I looked around the room. I didn't know anyone aside from Ang. She was flipping through a magazine. *Love your neighbor*. I just said that to Angie before we came to the hospital. How ironic I'd hear it now from a medic.

"So Doc, when are you coming back to men's Bible study? We miss you."

"I know. My schedule didn't allow it for a while, and then

I got in the habit of not coming. But I acknowledge the need for iron sharpening iron, accountability. I know I'm a better person when I'm in fellowship. I'll be there this Thursday, Pete." They shook hands.

Pete? Why did that ring a bell. No, it's the voice. A tingle ran down my spine. The voice rings a bell. I looked over at the doctor and he smiled. The medic turned around and then I saw the fireman's mustache, the glacier blue eyes, the dark tanned skin — Pete?

I stood up. "Excuse me? Pete? From Vegas?"

The doctor held up a hand. "Wait a minute. Pete? Vegas? Is there something you need to confess? I'm confused."

"Amelia? What? I thought you lived in Alaska? What are you doing here?" He looked me over. "Oh, you've been hurt. What happened?"

"I do. Live in Alaska, I mean. I'm just visiting a friend. No, I'm not hurt — at least not recently. What are you doing here? I thought you lived in Vegas? You said you were going to Portland to visit your daughter."

"I was in Vegas for a conference. I stopped to see my daughter on my way back here."

"Then why are you so tan?" I had no idea why I'd asked that. The moment felt surreal, yet I felt my face grow hot, and probably as red as a firetruck — a confirmation that the moment was embarrassingly real.

Pete laughed then looked back to the doctor. "You know what? I'm kind of confused too." He looked at me. "If you were wondering about my tan, why didn't you email me and ask?"

"Because I thought you lived in Vegas and it's hot and sunny and tan friendly there. And very noisy, I might add."

Angie stood and touched my arm. "You know, Mel, I'm kind of confused too. Do you two know each other?"

"Yes. No. I mean we met when I was at a conference in

Vegas. Remember when I had to text because it was too noisy to talk on the phone? We met on my return flight. Or rather we were seated next to each other and he kind of rescued me. I guess that's what he does for a living." I nodded toward his uniform. "Rescue people." I looked at Pete and his smile reached his eyes. He was actually handsome.

The doctor said, "Well this has been quite interesting but I gotta run because you guys keep bringing me patients to take care of. But Pete, we have to have coffee and catch up. Soon."

"We'll do that Doc. Give me a call. How about Thursday after Bible study?"

"Works for me. See you then." He patted Pete on the shoulder and waved at me.

Pete turned back to me and said, "What happened to your leg?"

"I slipped on the ice. Broke my ankle but it's a clean break."

"I'm sorry. Wish I'd been there to catch you."

I felt my face heat up again.

"How long are you here for? Maybe we can get together?"

I felt like a teenaged girl. What was it about this man? "I'm sorry but today is my last day in town. I fly out in the morning."

"How interesting that our paths would cross again like two ships in the night. Like maybe it's not a coincidence?" He raised an eyebrow. "Well, it's been nice to see you. And you can email anytime, you have my email address. I hope you heal soon." He reached out and touched my arm. "God bless you. And I hope you'll email me."

I nodded. "Good to see you, Pete. Surprising, but good. And God bless you too."

~

We stayed at the hospital until Mr. Stroud was taken to a room in telemetry and settled. He was communicating well, and was able to give the nurse his son's phone number. He gave Angie his apartment key and she offered to take care of his cat while he was in the hospital.

Angie and I sang along to a worship song on the radio while driving back to her apartment early that evening. When it ended she said, "So are you going to email him?"

"I'm trying to process what happened. Do you think it's just a coincidence? I mean that of all the places in the world two strangers could be, they'd be in the same place at the same moment? Twice? Okay, I guess he lives in Seattle, but even at that we were in the same place at the same moment. And I acted like a school girl, what's with that? There's just something about him — I guess I'm intrigued."

She laughed. "Well, he was a man in uniform and not a bad looking one either. He seemed happy to see you. His face lit up. He's obviously older than you but maybe mature enough to know what he wants. And to appreciate it when he gets it? So are you going to email him?"

"I — no."

"What? Why not?"

"Ang, I don't have his email address."

"But he said you did."

"He gave it to me when we were getting off of our flight. A really obnoxious drunk was sitting on the aisle and I was in the middle seat. Pete said he had to use the restroom and when he came back he had me move to the window so the guy couldn't bother me. Pete was really nice to me, but when I went to board my next flight I figured why would I ever want to email a guy in Vegas, and I tossed it."

"In the trash?"

"No, in the air! Of course in the trash. Well, I guess he

doesn't have to worry about me cluttering up his inbox." I hit my head with the palm of my hand and groaned.

"Would you really email him if you had it?"

"Doesn't make any difference. I don't have it." I smiled but knew it didn't reach my eyes.

Angie glanced over at me. "You like him, don't you?"

"I don't even know him." I looked out my window and watched the landscape go by. "I will admit that I see some qualities in him that I find — attractive.

"Maybe God put you here today to help Mr. Stroud."

"One never knows."

"Or maybe God put you here to help Mr. Stroud so you could run into Pete?"

I laughed. "You think? And to let me know that maybe I shouldn't have tossed that email address in the trash?"

Angie laughed. "One never knows."

"I have to admit that it is a little weird that he and I have met — twice."

"If it's meant to be maybe you'll meet a third time." She giggled.

"I seriously doubt that. And besides I have my own plans in place — they've just been a little delayed. I 'm sure that running into him was a coincidence, that's all." I heard the assured words from my mouth, but a trace of doubt lingered in the back of my mind.

While Angie went to Mr. Stroud's apartment to make sure his cat was okay, I packed my carry-on, except for a nightgown and toiletries which I'd pack in the morning. When she came back we sat on the sofa — Angie with her tea and me with a bottle of water.

"We never ate dessert yesterday! We need to have it now or I'll have to eat it all by myself with Mr. Stroud not home."

"I agree. You don't need all that goodness for yourself. We

laughed and took our angel food cake with strawberries and whipped cream back to the living room to eat.

Angie said, "This has been a crazy, fast visit. Time seems to zip by when we're together."

"It has gone by too quickly, yet it's been fun. And eventful to say the least. Thank you for opening up your home."

"Mi casa es su casa. You're family, Mel. My home is always open to you. What time do I have to release you to the handsome Dr. Fletcher tomorrow?" Her face crinkled in a grin.

"He's supposed to be here about nine, and he'll call when he gets close. You have whipped cream on your chin. And what is that grin about?"

She giggled and wiped her chin with her napkin. "Oh, here you are writing a romance novel yet you don't date. But if you did I think I know of two fellas who would definitely be interested in taking you out."

"Stop that, Ang. Now you sound like the kids I work with. They're always trying to set me up. Funny that they think they can see what's good for me, but they are either in bad relationships or none at all. It's always easier to diagnose someone else, I guess."

Even though we stayed up until nearly midnight talking, I had showered by six fifteen and was getting dressed when I heard Angie turn on the shower.

I went to the kitchen and pulled fruit and cream cheese from her refrigerator that we had left over from lunch yesterday. I put the tea kettle on to heat for her tea. She came into the kitchen, her damp hair almost in ringlets.

"Ah you look like a little girl with those curls. It's cute."

She laughed. "I've been using a straightener forever. You get to see me in my natural state. I need to straighten it before I go to work."

"Why? What's wrong with curls? It's a lot easier to leave it natural isn't it?"

"You know, maybe I will for today then I can have break-fast with you before I head to work instead of standing in front of the bathroom mirror for twenty-five minutes." She grabbed a couple of plates. "Where's the breadsticks?"

"You want them for breakfast? I put them in the microwave."

She set them on the table and set a tea ball in a china cup. "You sure you don't want to try some tea, Mel?"

"Never. Thanks. What else can I get you for breakfast? Want me to cook you an egg or something?"

"You're so good to me. No, I'm taking some leftovers for lunch. I'll eat well today on the food we prepared the last couple of days. I wish I could stay till you leave, but I need to be at work for a meeting this morning."

"And I kept you up late last night."

"No, I kept you up late last night. I'm going to miss you. When Mitch picks you up will you just lock the door on your way out?"

"Will do." We gave thanks for our food and ate in silence, enjoying the presence of each other's company. We'd been friends for years and one of the things we were both grateful for is that we could fill the space with chatter or just be quiet together.

An hour after Angie hugged me goodbye, Mitch called. "I'm about fifteen minutes away. Do you need more time than that to get ready?"

"I've been ready for hours. Ang is at work and I'm packed. See you in a few. I'll watch for you and meet you out front."

"What about your carry-on and crutches?"

"I'm fine. I can carry both. See you."

On the drive to the airport, I asked Mitch about his ski weekend. I had to smile at how animated he became — like my sons would when they spoke about anything they were passionate about. "I'm glad you had fun, Mitch. Skiing obviously brings you pleasure."

"What about your weekend? Lots of hallmark movies and girl talk?"

"That sounds about right." Then I shared about the fish hawker at Pike's Market Place, brunch at the Silver Porche and the episode with Mr. Stroud, although I didn't mention Pete.

Mitch and I were again seated in first class. Fortunately we didn't run into anyone from work. We chatted while the flight attendant served food and drinks. I leaned back in my seat and found it difficult to keep my eyes open. I drifted off and saw Pete standing there smiling at me. "Why didn't you write?" I startled and sat up.

"Are you okay?"

"Yes, I guess I dozed off. Late night."

"Your head was on my shoulder. I nearly dozed off myself until you jumped."

My face grew warm. "I'm sorry." I leaned toward the window just in case I dozed off again.

"I didn't mind." He smiled. "You can lean on me anytime."

Our flight landed and Mitch took my carry-on along with his own as we made our way through the terminal. "I'll take your bag and go get the car. Meet you in front of baggage claim?"

"Okay. Thanks, Mitch." I avoided looking around because I'd never been to the airport without seeing at least one person I knew.

"Mel, where are you returning from?"

I turned to see the pastor's wife from church. At least it wasn't someone from work. "Hi, Tessa. I've been in Seattle visiting a friend."

"What happened to you?" She nodded towards my boot.

"I slipped on the ice. I'll get this boot off in a couple of weeks. How are things with you?"

"Oh you know — busy, busy. Hope we see you soon."

I saw Mitch pull up. "I hope so too." I gave her a one armed hug. "My ride is here. Tell Steven hello."

"I will." She walked with me to the door and I saw her look to see who was driving.

Mitch got out of the car and came around to open the door for me. He turned and waved at Tessa before he walked back to the drivers side and got in.

"Do you know Tessa and Steven, Mitch?"

"Nope." He grinned.

I shook my head. *Does he do things like that on purpose?*

My phone rang while I tossed clothes in the wash. "Hey, Margie, how's your day going?"

"So far, so good. Did you make it home okay?"

"Yes, I got here about an hour ago. Thank you for taking care of the critters while I was gone. It was a whirlwind trip and I'm so glad I got to go."

"How'd you get home from the airport?"

Jack Frost barked. "Oh, I think someone's here. Gotta go. See you next week." I hung up and looked over at Jack. "So you need some attention? You got it. Thank you for giving me an excuse to get off the phone." He wagged his tail and I rubbed his ears.

Maybe people would be asking questions at work, but for now I'd avoid the witness stand.

I made a list of things I needed to do before I sorted the mail on the counter and checked my email.

Fast Eddy's picture was interesting. He wore an unbuttoned shirt and a large gold necklace that matched his upper front two teeth. *You're a lady after my own heart. Lamborghini, eh? I just happen to sell high end cars so I can relate to your appreciation for the finer things in life. Message me your phone number and I will take you for a ride. Yessir, honey, I think we will get along like a fine tuned engine. Hear me ROAR!*

I laughed so hard that it took three tries to copy and paste my standard reply. *Seriously?*

CHAPTER 11

*M*y first day back to work I had mixed feelings. According to my original timeline, I would have had a cottage being built in Idaho right now, but I hadn't even met with a contractor and spring wasn't far off. Oh, how I knew that Alaska could titillate her inhabitants this time of year — whispering the promise of spring. The air would change and when she had people chasing, trying to grab hold, she would turn a cold shoulder and watch them scatter for coats and warm fires again. When she decided spring would arrive, she painted hope on the trees in the form of tiny green buds. People watched closely, morning and evening to see the first buds open.

My decision to move was set in stone and I was ready for change, making it difficult to return to my job. I went straight to the locker room to change into scrubs before making my way to the coffee kiosk. Debbie greeted me with a big smile. "Welcome back, stranger. So I bet you have some tales to tell."

"Good morning, Debbie. Few tales here. How about you?"

She made my usual and handed it to me. "You're not going to tell me anything?"

I took my drink and put a straw in it. "What's to tell? Have a great day."

I walked back to the ER and realized there'd been plenty of time for rumors to get out of hand since seeing Skip on the flight to Seattle. I groaned. *Lord, I don't want to deal with gossip today. Help me to be full of grace.*

Ellen entered the ER the same time as me. It relieved me to see her because she was sensible and not prone to talking about other people. "Good morning, Ellen. I'm so glad to see you."

She greeted me with a hug. "It's good to have you back. Funny how one part of the team being gone seems to throw everything off a little."

"Is everything okay?"

"Yes, but I missed working with you and it gave me a taste for what it will be like after you move."

"Well, I can take you with me when I move." I smiled at her.

"I wish. But I don't think I'll ever get my husband to travel outside of Alaska let alone move." She laughed.

Throughout the day various people made comments, asked questions or insinuated they knew something.

I managed to side step questions by doing my job and ignored the rest. Really, I didn't come to work and ask them about their private lives. Did people have no boundaries at all?

Seven hours into my shift, Mitch came on duty. Fortunately, I was busy with a patient and didn't have time to exchange pleasantries in front of coworkers. Shortly before the end of my shift I had to assist him with a female patient. When he went out of the room to write up orders, I helped her get dressed.

"Something going on with you and the handsome doctor?"

"We work together."

"But you agree he's handsome? You're not blind."

"Yes, I suppose he is."

"I think he likes you too. But if you don't want him, I'll take him." She laughed coarsely. I finished with her, washed my hands and went to check on one of my other patients. Katy came in shortly to take the patient to radiology. "Mel, long time no see. I hear you went on a little *ski* trip. How was it?" She made a surprised face and laughed.

"You misheard. I went to Seattle to spend a few days with a friend." I smiled at the patient and placed a warm blanket over him for his excursion to radiology.

Katy seemed frustrated that she wasn't getting any information. "I'll return your patient as soon as I can."

The medic phone rang and Ellen answered. After she handed the note to Dr. Fletcher, she told me we had a GSW arriving in about nine minutes. Gun shot wounds weren't an every day event in our ER like some places, but they got our adrenaline pumping. Ours weren't gang related — rather most commonly accidents or attempted suicides. It wasn't hunting season so the accident prospect was reduced this time.

When the medics arrived all the staff was on hand waiting. Respiratory, lab, radiology, doctor, nurses, techs, pharmacy and nursing supervisor who was Sheila. As the medic gave his report, we took our places around the patient. I started an IV and respiratory staff handled the Ambu bag, Grace stepped up on the stool ready to do CPR and Ellen was cutting the patients' shirt off. The wound turned out to be in his upper abdomen.We quickly spotted the entrance of the bullet, but we found no exit wound. We paged the surgeon and the patient was transferred to surgery.

At the end of my shift I emailed the ER manager to request vacation days to go to Idaho. I wasn't sure how she'd feel about it after me being off for six weeks with my ankle. But I had a fair amount of vacation accrued and if I didn't take it, I would get it in pay when I resigned. And I had to get to Idaho to meet with the contractor and get my cottage started. And meet with the hospital HR folks.

The next morning I had a message from Out of Africa.

Dear Sweet Lady, Come with me and I'll show you the elephants. I'm a medical missionary to Africa, caring for prisoners and orphans. I'm not into games and I'm looking for a woman who is ready to Go, Love, Serve. It's you — if you have a heart for sharing Jesus and are willing to work alongside His servant. If you want to be treasured and loved in a fully committed relationship — write me.

I read the letter three times. I didn't feel like I could copy and paste my standard reply to this man. There was so much more to him. Someone who was willing to go places I'd certainly never go. I shut my laptop and vacuumed and dusted the house. Later in the morning I returned to my office to write a short note to the missionary.

Dear Out of Africa, thank you for writing. What organization do you serve with in Africa? Are you with a group? How long have you been working there? I'm sure you have seen things I will never see. I have friends through my church that are missionaries so have heard stories. I hold them and you in high regard. One lady is single, perhaps I should tell her I've come across someone she could write to?

I've heard the call to dinner, the mountains, the river and work, but never the call to Africa. Be blessed. — Crystal

That evening I made my lunch for the next day since I was scheduled to work. On my way to bed I wrote a quick email to each of my sons. My inbox pinged.

Dear Crystal,

I've worked in Africa for fourteen years — intermittently — because I have to return to the states to work in order to fund my work in Africa, and also to keep up my credentials. There are organizations and local pastors I work alongside, but I'm currently not 'sent' by a church. I'm sent by God.

By the way, you don't need to tell your single missionary friend about me. It's your profile that caught my attention.

Have you read Jon Piper's book, 'Let the Nations Be Glad'? 'The Hole in Our Gospel' by Richard Stearns (he's the CEO of World Vision). Also 'Radical' by David Platt?

Being curious and an avid reader, I went to the website of my favorite bookstore and ordered the books before I went to bed. Before I went to sleep, I wondered what 'Out of Africa' looked like. It didn't matter. He was someone who was passionate about God and I could be a pen pal. I'd had pen pals as a child and even during Desert Storm I'd written to soldiers and sent care packages.

My curiosity was stirred by Out of Africa's email. I went back to the site to look at his profile. It said there were photos so I clicked to open them. I almost felt like I was spying. The pictures were obviously taken in Africa where he was surrounded by smiling children. I couldn't really tell what he looked like with the safari hat shading his face from the sun. But it didn't matter. I was getting a glimpse into his heart and knew we could be pen pals.

I saw Mitch pull into the doctors parking as I parked in the lot out near the street. He waited and walked in with me. Gil came running up behind us and put a hand on each of our shoulders.

"Hey guys, what's happening?"

"You are," Mitch answered.

"So is there anything you two want to confide to me?"

I looked at Mitch and we both laughed. "I'm sure it would be a secret for at least ten seconds, don't you think so, Dr. Fletcher?"

"Oh, I'm certain of it. Here's the scoop, Gil. We're going to go inside and heal people."

"Man, you guys are a wall."

I said, "We are separate walls, not *A* wall, Gil." He trailed us inside like a scolded puppy. Dr. Fletcher went to the doctor's locker room, and I patted Gil on the shoulder. Get changed and I'll buy you a coffee.

"Really? I'll be out in a flash."

"No, don't flash — put your scrubs on."

He laughed. "Okay, gotcha."

Mitch signaled me over during a lull after a busy morning. "Amelia, would you ask everyone what they'd like? I'm buying pizza for the crew today for working so well as a team." He handed me his credit card.

"Sure, that's sweet of you. What kind do you like?"

The ER manager took a couple pieces of pizza then handed me an envelope from her pocket. I opened it up to find my leave request approved. On my break I got on the internet to book a flight, and then I made a list of things to do. Reserve a hotel room, line up a rental car, call the hospitals to make appointments with HR, and contact the contractor. The rest of the day the my giddiness was mistaken by coworkers as either a caffeine high or love. *Let them think what they will.*

That night I had three new messages from Strike a Match. Radio Man wrote; *Hi there, Crystal. I'm a DJ on your favorite radio station. At least it should be your favorite. I like to travel and would love to have someone who's like minded. We can even share a room — to save money of course. Wink. Wink. I'm told I have a sexy voice. I'd like to hear what you think.*

I looked at his photo to see if was as brassy as he sounded. He had actually winked at the camera. "You don't really want to know what I think, Radio Man." I copied and pasted my standard reply.

The next was a letter from Out of Africa. *Dear Crystal, Forgive me, but I have been thinking about you. The fact that you responded to me tells a lot about you. Most women would not even bother once they read the part about going to Africa. The ones that have, tried to convince me I should forget about Africa and come to them and live on their terms. One woman actually wrote that she was still married but looking for someone better suited to her. Can you believe that? Your profile said you had lived in a cabin with no water or electricity. I haven't met another woman who could say that — aside from missionaries.*

Dear Out of Africa, Yes, I can believe it. There are some unique folks on this site, for sure. I ordered the books you mentioned. I hadn't heard of any of them but I read all the time. I'll let you know what I think. Have a good week.

I closed my email. I didn't feel like reading any more messages. My phone rang and I saw that it was Robert Ide.

"Hello, Robert."

"Good evening, Amelia, I hope you're doing well. Hey, I have someone interested in seeing your house. When can I bring them by?"

I was taken by surprise. Robert hadn't shown the house yet and with my broken ankle and all the delays for my move I was glad. The timing was interesting now that I was about to go to Idaho to get the ball rolling. Well, God's timing is perfect.

"Is this weekend good for them? I'll be at work. Remember I do have a dog and cat. Should you bring them when I can take the critters out of the house?"

"No, they are fine. Your house is so clean, you don't need to worry about that. You should see some of the places I've seen. Your house will show very well. Will Saturday work?"

"Yes, I'll be at work. Will you let me know what they think?"

"Of course. I'll leave my card on the kitchen counter so you know I was there and I'll text or call and let you know."

This was getting really real now. The house was about to be shown and I was going to Idaho. Everything was moving forward. All of a sudden I felt like a kid when I'd made the long trek up a sledding hill and now I was bracing for the fast ride down.

When the books arrived in the mail I started with *Let the Nations Be Glad.* The consensus was about giving God His Glory. I couldn't put it down and had read the first five chapters before I took a break. It wasn't like the information was new to me, but I felt challenged. The next day I read *Radical.* Again I felt challenged.

I got home Saturday evening from work and found Robert's card on the kitchen counter. Everything looked fine and the critters didn't seem upset, so all must have gone well. I checked my email and found my car rental and hotel reservation confirmations. I had two weeks to get ready for this trip.

Dear Out of Africa, I've been reading the books you suggested and I have to say you're challenging me. I knew much of what I've read, but see it in a new light. I believe in the Scripture and take to heart Colossians 3:23 — to do everything as though I'm doing it for the Lord. That's how I approach life, yet it seems there's more. Not just doing everything for Him, but to do it for His Glory.

Monday morning I called Margie. "Good morning, did I wake you?"

She yawned. "No, I just haven't had any coffee yet."

"Margie, I've got all my reservations for the trip I had to

cancel a couple months ago. Are you still up for staying at my house?"

"I'd be happy to." She sounded more awake now.

"There's one challenge though. I listed the house with a real estate agent and he showed it on Saturday. If he needs to show it, you'd have to vacate before he arrives. I could give him your number and he could text or call you and tell you when he's coming and when they leave. If it's not too much trouble."

"That's okay. Do you think he'll show it much?"

"I have no idea. It's only been shown once so far. He's good about screening potential buyers to make sure it fits what they're looking for and he only shows to those who have been pre-approved."

"Just let me know when you need me to come. And don't forget to make food." She laughed.

"I would not forget to feed my favorite critter sitter. Thank you, Margie."

Dear Lovely Woman of God, if you feel challenged, it's not me, but the Holy Spirit. He has a way of speaking to our hearts. Do you agree? Have you ever had strong leanings about something and then felt guided in another direction and saw that it turned out for the best? It might not have been what you would have chosen because you couldn't see the whole picture when you were making your choice. I certainly have experienced that myself. And there were times I ran ahead and went my own way and it turned out disastrous. Yes, I'm a fallible human being. :) Blessings.

I recalled the conversation Ang and I had about seeing God's plan. Interesting that this man seemed to be on the same page.

I went to town to run some errands and pick up some groceries. I thought I'd cook a few meals to put in the freezer for Margie while she critter sat. I bought cinnamon chips to make her oatmeal cookies because I remembered her mentioning those were her favorite. Then I picked up some more flour so I could make cinnamon rolls to take to work. The crew would enjoy those. I stopped by the post office to drop off bills then remembered I'd wanted to pick up a real estate flyer to see my listing. I pulled into the parking lot of the nearest store where I knew they had flyers in the entryway. I ran in and grabbed one and heard someone say my name.

"Oh hi, Dr. Martinez. You out spending all your hard earned money on sporting goods?"

He chuckled. "No, but I'm dreaming about hunting season. That's the best part."

"I'm sure. No near misses in a dream."

"So you're really going to go looking for work out of state?"

"No secrets in this town, are there?"

"I thought you and Mitch had something going on?"

"And what would that be?"

"You two just seem to go together. He's a good guy. And you're a sweet woman."

"Well, thank you. But I'm not really looking to be in a relationship. I'm happily single and have my life planned out. I'm excited about the season I'm entering. I think Mitch is a good guy too, truly. I need to run — have a lot to do. Oh, I'm baking cinnamon rolls for the gang."

"I'll see you at work, Mel. Make sure you save me a big cinnamon roll."

I smiled and waved on my way out the door.

Dear Out of Africa, I confess I too have gone boldly where I shouldn't have gone. And the heartache and shame that resulted were the punishment I brought on myself. My hearts desire is to serve God, but my attitude sometimes doesn't reveal that. Then I find myself on my knees asking for forgiveness — again. God is so gracious and merciful. When I think He should ignore my pleas, He instead brings me comfort. My ambition is to be an ambassador of Christ. To take Him wherever I go and live in a way that honors Him. To love others as He commands and I must confess I fall terribly short sometimes. I feel like a puppy sometimes — wanting to please my master by bringing him his slippers but then I stop and chew on them first. Ah — the battle of the flesh. Blessings.

I decided to list my furniture for sale. All aside from my twin bed. I could live without the rest if it sold now and then I wouldn't have to take pennies for it when it was time to move just to get rid of it. The first day my ad ran, I got a call about my cherry wood dining room set. I arranged for the lady and her husband to come on Saturday in case they purchased it because he'd be off work and could drive his pickup to get it home. I looked around the house. I didn't need my china now. I wouldn't be hosting any special meals before I moved. I made a list of things in the kitchen that I had to sell, then settled on a fair asking price for each item. I went through every room of my house and made a separate list. I'd have to get some boxes to put things in to make it easier for people to take the smaller things home. I wrote that on my list of things to do next time I went to town.

I stopped to watch a bull moose in my front yard. He was so beautiful. Chickadees flew over his head and landed on my bird feeder to eat the black oil sunflower seeds. A small wave of sadness washed over me. I would miss Alaska terribly.

I didn't even try to stop the tear that traced down my cheek and it was soon followed by another. I let the emotion come and waited for it to pass.

Father, I will never tire of the beauty of your creation. And I know that all creation has been formed by your hand, so no matter where I go, I will see you there.

I stood silently for some minutes, until Snowball wove around my legs. I looked down and she turned her little head up and purred. I picked her up and kissed her ear. "You are some of God's handiwork, little princess. You are indeed."

Although I usually kept my home clean and pretty clutter free, there was still quite a lot to go through once all the cupboards and closets were opened. I was glad I hadn't waited until after going to Idaho to do this job. I would have been overwhelmed — because this wasn't just a move from my house — it was a complete new beginning.

The lady who had called about my dining room set showed up on Saturday morning as planned. She definitely wanted the set and asked about the china hutch.

"Everything is for sale. I've been listing it all a little at a time so if you're interested in anything just say so."

She looked over at her husband and he nodded. "Your furniture is just lovely. How can you part with it all?"

"I'm moving outside of Alaska and I'm single. Trying to figure out how to move everything was overwhelming. This is the easiest way for me to move. Fresh start."

She followed her husband outside to get blankets to wrap around the furniture. When they came back in she said, "We'll take the china hutch too. We moved up here not long ago for my husbands job and the moving company ended up destroying some of our furniture. This was perfect timing for us." As they carried the furniture out she noticed my snake plant by the fireplace. "That's beautiful, and huge. You must have had that for quite a while."

"Yes, I bought it as a little thing — I wanted something on the hearth that would grow without blocking the hallway."

"The pot is beautiful too. Are you going to sell your plants?"

"Yes, I'm only taking what will fit in my car."

"Wow. I'd like to buy it. I love houseplants."

I got some plastic garbage bags and we wrapped the plant in those to protect it before they carried it out and placed it in the backseat of their extended cab. "Do you like spider plants?"

"Yes, I had one before we moved here."

I pulled a chair over to the one I had hanging in the living room and took it down. "Welcome to Alaska. Here's a house-warming gift for you."

"Are you serious?"

"Yes, my plants are kind of like my kids. I'm happy it will go where it's appreciated."

I got some more plastic garbage bags and we wrapped the plant up and carried it out together. Her husband counted out cash to me for the total of the items they'd purchased. I trusted them but it was nice not to have to go cash a check.

After they left I got a call from a lady inquiring about my sofa.

"If you can come this afternoon that'd be great. Otherwise I won't have time to show it to you until Wednesday."

"I can be there within the hour. I hope you don't sell it before I come."

"I'm showing my furnishings by appointment only so you're good."

While I waited for her to come, I sorted through my closet. Since I rarely wore anything besides scrubs and jeans, I didn't have many clothes to go through, but I went through them just the same. I didn't need my old painting clothes since I was going to buy a house newly built. I put those in a rag pile. It only took a few minutes to finish in my closet and I heard a car coming up the driveway.

"This is exactly what I have been looking for. It's Amish made?"

"Yes, it is."

"I looked at this very sofa in Anchorage and they were asking almost three times what you're asking."

"I know what store you're talking about. I saw it there

too, but found a company in the lower forty-eight who offered me free shipping."

"I'd like to buy the chair and coffee table too. I've had mismatched furniture forever. It will be so nice to have a set. Oh! That painting is beautiful. Who did it?"

I looked down at the floor. "Thank you. Actually I painted it."

She went over to look closer. "Is it for sale?"

"That's not for sale. My granddaughter loves that painting. I'm saving it for her."

"Lucky girl. Okay, what's my total?"

I added up the price for the sofa, chair and coffee table and gave her the figure.

"That's an amazing deal. Thank you. I'm so excited. Let me write you a check and I'm going to call my husband and have him bring a friend with his truck so we can get everything at once."

"That sounds great. I've been baking cookies. Would you like some while you wait?"

She laughed. "Why not?"

She followed me into the kitchen. I pulled out the container of cookies and offered her water or tea. She chose tea. I heated the water and got a china cup down. "Do you care for cream or sugar? I have honey as well."

"A little honey would be great. This cup is gorgeous. Are you selling your china too?"

I pictured how much space I'd have in my car. "Yes, I guess I will be selling it."

CHAPTER 12

On Sunday I carried the cinnamon rolls into work and set them in the break room on my way to the locker room. I got my scrubs on and looked in the mirror as I pulled my hair up with a scrunchy. I stopped and tried to picture my hair cut short. I couldn't imagine it. I went to the coffee kiosk to get a drink before I clocked in. The morning started out quietly so I used the time to check inventory and do a bit of stocking. A patient came in, but Ellen had them covered so I kept at my task.

Later while everyone was enjoying a cinnamon roll, the medic phone rang. I didn't have any cinnamon roll in my mouth so I answered. "ER, this Mel."

"ER, this is medic 1 and we are inbound with a twenty-six-year-old male involved in an MVA, complaining of leg pain. ETA five minutes."

"Room four on arrival, medic 1." I handed the note to Dr. Martinez and went to ready room four. When I came out of the room I heard the medic phone ring again.

Josh answered it. "ER, this is Josh."

"Okay, I'll open the ambulance bay. Meet you there." As

we passed he said, "Hey Mel, want to grab a wheelchair? Troopers are bringing in a couple of guys for substance abuse testing. Not sure if they are upright or not."

"Gotcha." I grabbed a wheelchair and met Josh in the ambulance bay. The troopers were unloading a couple of younger men — both in handcuffs. I stood by with the wheelchair and one of the young men began flailing and trying to kick the officer as well as Josh.

Josh was tall with broad shoulders — he appeared to be quite a bit larger than the man in cuffs, but the patient wasn't intimidated. He cursed and kicked and tried to wrangle away from the men who were trying to get him safely into the wheelchair for transport.

Josh held out his hand. "Stay back, Mel."

I nodded. I didn't want to put myself in danger either. It was pretty obvious that the substance test was in order. I left the wheelchair and returned to the department, praying for all concerned as I went. Later, after talking with the troopers, we pieced together what had taken place. The young man brought in with a leg injury was actually involved with the other two in a drug encounter. When it went bad, he tried to stop them and they hit him with the car they were driving. He was fortunate as nothing was broken — he'd only have a bruise.

Trooper Lamb accepted my offer of a cinnamon roll.

"You guys have to deal with some awful stuff. I pray for your safety. It's not like you can reason with a person on mind altering substances. We've had a few in here. One day I was taking a patient to a room and when the surgical nurse and I were transferring her to the bed, she dropped her purse and all her paraphernalia rolled across the floor."

"Mel, it's like there are two worlds out there and we try to keep them separate. Occasionally we fail and then you see the *stuff* you saw today."

"Yes, we get to see the underside in the ER, for sure. We all want to help people and make a difference, but there are some folks only God can help."

"You got that right. And He only can if they'll let Him." He reached out and touched my shoulder. "Keep the faith, Mel."

"You too. Be safe."

Later on Josh came out and grabbed the bottle of peppermint oil. He opened it and dabbed some under his nose.

"Gotta a ripe one, Josh?"

He rolled his eyes. "Man, this dude needs a shower but I can't handle getting him in there. I considered wearing an hazmat mask but thought it might be over the top."

I laughed. How big of a guy? I'll go find some clothes and you can put the ones he's wearing in a burn bag."

"A medium guy. Do you think we have any coats?"

"I know we do. I sorted and organized all that stuff a couple of weeks ago. Go get the man in front of a fire hose and I'll get his gear."

Josh laughed. "Now that's an idea."

By the time I left work that evening, I felt emotionally drained. Not drained like I'd have felt if we'd had seriously injured or sick people. Taking care of them was rewarding, but dealing with people who seemed to live to make bad choices and didn't seem to have any desire to change — there was no fulfillment at the end of the day. Those kinds of days left me with little gratification with my job.

When I got home, I turned the water on to take a shower. I stood under the soothing, hot water longer than usual. After getting my pajamas on, I sliced up an apple and pepper jack cheese then sat on the rug on the living room floor.

The room seemed so big and empty with most of the furniture and two of my larger plants gone. I ate my snack, brushed my teeth and decided to lie in bed and read since there was no chair to sit in. For some reason I couldn't focus on my book so got up and got my laptop.

Dear Godly Lady, I was reading my Bible this morning and kept seeing your smiling face. I sense there is hurt behind that smile. You're on a relationship site, but are you truly looking for someone? I am honored that you communicate with me. I'm attracted to the genuine heart for God that I see in your letters. Your openness to new ideas, and discussion. And a sense of adventure. I'm stepping out on a limb here, but I will be leaving for Africa again in about three weeks. Would it be possible to buy you lunch or dinner? I would so love to talk to you in person, my friend.

I read his letter over. He seemed to have read between the lines. I hadn't really shared anything with him, but he knew. How did he know? He's going back to Africa. I just as well be honest with him.

Dear Out of Africa, I find it uncanny what you seem to pick up through my letters. You are right — there was a deep hurt. I've been too ashamed to even share it with anyone. My husband was killed in an accident. A young teenaged boy was also killed with him. Drugs and paraphernalia were found in the car. It turned out I didn't know the man I had been married to at all. And when he was killed I knew I'd never know the answers to the many questions I had about the distance and coldness in our relationship.

The accident reports were in the newspaper so I couldn't protect my sons, who also were left with many unanswered questions. We all had to deal with the information on our own terms. My younger son fled to Europe. I knew he felt shame as heavily as I did. I sought counseling, and from that and the Word, was able to separate myself from the shame that wasn't mine to carry.

I quit my job and found work in another area away from the people that had seen me walking in humiliation and pain. I don't know why I feel I can trust you with all of this — except I'm healed and whole now. And sharing the truth is like the period at the end of the healing sentence. Bless you, my friend.

I released a deep sigh, set my laptop on the floor and stretched. I hung my arm off the side of my bed to pet Jack's ears. I heard his tail hit the floor softly in response. "Good night, sweet boy."

When I woke up and looked at the clock I was shocked that I had slept for over eight hours. That only happened when I was sick, but I didn't feel sick. I must have really been exhausted. I got up and did my morning routine. It felt strange to see all the space in my house. It made me want to move sooner because I felt like I didn't belong here.

After eating a bite, I decided to try to work on my book. I checked Strike a Match.

Thomas wrote; *Hi Crystal. What town do you live in? I travel with my pharmaceutical sales job and would like to hook up with you on my way through.*

I had to think about that proposal for a half second. *Hook up? Are you kidding me? Did you read my profile, bonehead?* I copied and pasted my standard reply. The letter was an insult and I was duly insulted. I supposed I must be really old fashioned. When did that happen? *Hook up?* Good grief, guy — they have special sites just for your kind. I shook my head and shut down my laptop. Actually from many of the responses I'd gotten, I didn't think most of them bothered with reading the profile. Good thing I wasn't looking at theirs either. I imagined it'd be like wading in a kiddie pool. SHALLOW.

~

I'd made so many lists over the last few months since I decided to move. Well, I'd always made lists, but lately I'd had lists on steroids. Since my ads had been published I'd sold all my furniture including my twin bed — but I kept my mattress. My clothes were now in boxes instead of a dresser.

The lady who'd bought my living room furniture was delighted when I called and gave her my price for the china. She picked it up that day. She brought a friend who bought my silver and several crystal items. My office desk was gone along with the lamps and lamp tables.

I still had my rug. I'd had offers on it, but decided to keep it. It would roll up and fit in my car nicely and at least I'd have something in my hew home to sit on until I could find things at yard sales or in ads. I had to laugh at myself. For so many years I'd saved up to buy high quality furnishings and once I let them go, I wasn't worried about replacing them with more fine things. Something is changing — me — I'm changing. I'm not sure how, but I can sense it.

Dear *Precious Pearl, I read your letter with tears. I'm so sorry for the pain that you and your sons endured. I've committed my own sins that hurt others and even though I asked them and God for forgiveness, I still have the regret.*

I can't tell you how honored I am that you were willing to open up to me. I don't know that I deserve that, but I'm so grateful to be allowed into your heart and confidence.

You didn't answer about allowing me to buy you lunch or dinner so I will leave that alone. And old guy can hope, can't he? But I will be more than happy to be your friend. We can write and pray for one another as a brother and sister in Christ, can we not? You deserve to be loved as Christ loved the church. To be treasured and valued for you are a pearl of great worth. See Matthew 14:46. Many blessings.

I did three walks through the house to make sure I hadn't forgotten to tie up any loose ends. This was part of my big move — a whole life change and I wavered between excitement and nervousness.

Dear Our of Africa, I haven't been completely honest with you. Please accept my apology. I can't imagine what you will think of me after I make this confession. I'm actually in Alaska. I'm sure you're wondering why I listed my location as Montana. I'm working on a book — a romantic comedy. I signed up on Strike a Match to do research. (You were right when you wrote that you wondered if I was truly seeking a match.) I wasn't trying to deceive you. In fact you are the only person I have written to. I felt I needed to since you were a missionary and seemed sincere in your walk with the Lord.

Now for another surprise. I'm actually moving to Idaho. My house is on the market and I'm going to Boise to meet with a contractor and a couple of HR department heads in two weeks. I'm so sorry for misleading you. I didn't intend to write anyone but have been so blessed by our correspondence. I understand if you don't write again. Although I will miss your letters. Blessings.

I started to sign my name as Crystal, but decided enough deception. I probably never should have written him in the first place and simply copied and pasted my response. Really what difference did it make now? I hoped I hadn't ruined his hopes for meeting someone willing to go work along side him. That would be sad since I had benefited from our correspondence. Reading the books he suggested had challenged me and I felt I'd grown in my walk with God.

As I packed my carry-on, Margie came in my room and sat on the floor.

"How many suitcases will you take?"

"Suitcases? None. I only travel with a carry-on. Makes life much simpler."

"I can't imagine having enough in that little bag to last a week. You're so organized."

"Well, there are some who tease me about being a little OCD, but I find that lists and organization make life much easier." I folded my three summer dresses and packed them with the undergarments I would wear with them. I folded shorts with shirts and undergarments to wear when I wasn't on business at the hospital.

Margie watched me and giggled. "I'm sorry that is just too organized. I'd never get packed if I did that. I just throw all my clothes in a suitcase, toss my makeup in a bag and grab another bag for whatever I forget to put in the first two."

"And you think that's easier than this?" I raised my eyebrows. I zipped the bag closed and set it next to the door and then sat down on my mattress. "Thank you again for taking care of things while I go, Margie. I really appreciate it. I feel bad that there isn't any furniture for you here. Are you really okay with that?"

"Hey, if you can live like this indefinitely, I can do it for a week." She laughed.

"And who knows, maybe some of your organization will rub off on me while I'm here."

"Who knows? Organization or minimalism?" I swept my hand around at the empty room. We both laughed.

That evening after arriving in Boise I picked up my rental car and drove to my hotel. With all the excitement of the day I didn't feel hungry so didn't bother stopping for dinner. I looked forward to a long, hot bath and a good nights sleep. Tomorrow would be a busy day between meeting with one of the Human Resource departments for a tour and a meeting with the contractor, Cliff.

I arrived at my first appointment twenty minutes early so I'd have time to park and find the HR department. I found a parking spot and walked to the main building. I stopped at the front desk and asked for directions, then headed down the hall. A tall, nice looking man in a suit stood down the hall speaking with another man. When he noticed me he smiled, and when I got close he put out his hand. "Are you looking for me?"

"Um, I don't think so. I think I'm meeting with a woman."

"Oh, okay."

I smiled. "I'm here to check out the ER. I'm a nurse."

"Hopefully I'll see you around then." He smiled.

"Maybe." I continued to the HR department, with growing anticipation.

Janet Carter came out of her office and extended her hand to me. "Amelia?"

"Yes, nice to meet you in person. I'm looking forward to seeing your hospital and meeting some of the employees."

She took me on a tour of the entire facility, with the emergency room being our last stop. When we arrived, the staff was working on a trauma patient, so she showed me the department herself. "Amelia, let me buy you something to drink and we'll chat a bit and come back so you can meet some of the staff."

The coffee kiosk was located in an open area with tables and chairs, floor to ceiling windows, and large plants. The colors and atmosphere were relaxing, which was intentional to calm waiting families, I was sure. By the time we returned to the ER, Janet had introduced me to the manager, a couple of the doctors and some of the nurses. All were congenial. I left feeling pretty good about the facility and the people that worked there.

I decided to grab a bite to eat before my appointment with Cliff. I hadn't eaten since yesterday. I noticed a cafe and a deli across the street from his office. I decided on the deli. There were a number of yummy looking breads to choose from, but I ordered a ham and cheese wrap and a bottle of water and sat down in a corner to watch people while I ate. There was a lively, friendly vibe to the place and I felt energized. I was almost done eating when my phone rang and I saw it was Tyson. I grabbed my purse, tossed the last of my wrap in the trash bin, and stepped outside.

"Tyson, honey it's so good to hear from you. Are you at Leightons'?"

"Not yet, I had some delays. That's why I'm calling. Were you planning to go to Wyoming too?"

"I was if you were going to be there."

"Oh good, I mean good that you're flexible. I talked to Leighton, and Jeannie is going to be over in Jackson Hole with the boys for some sports thing. They just found out about it."

"I have several things to take care of here in Boise, and since it sounds like we can't all get together this time, I'll just spend a bit more time getting familiar with this area. It won't be long before I'll be moving. I'm just happy that we will all be in the continental states together again. Or are you going back to Europe?"

"I think I'm sticking around. It's time to find gainful employment. I've been searching in all the wrong places."

"For?"

"Answers. And sometimes we just aren't going to know the answers. The folks who invited me to Germany are Christians. We had some good conversations while I was there and they helped me see some things more clearly. Like what Dad did may have hurt the rest of us, but it's not our burden to carry. And I was so angry at Dad, but I realized he's dead. My anger can't hurt him but it was tearing me up inside."

Thank you, Lord. Thank you for loving my son so much that you sent others to speak the Truth in love to him. Tears welled in my eyes.

"Mom? Did I lose you?"

"Oh no, honey, you haven't lost me. I'm here. And you

can't know what a gift this call is to me. I love you dearly and can't wait to see you — all in God's time."

"I love you too, Mom. You might give Leighton a call this evening."

"I will. You've made your Mom's heart sing." I couldn't stop smiling even while tears ran down my cheeks as I walked to my car. *People will think I'm nuts.* I got in my rental car and laughed a deep, wonderful laugh. I began singing the first song that came to mind, *Oh Come to the Alter*, by Elevation Worship.

~

Cliff showed me a few plans to see what I liked best. Some were the same ones he had already sent by email, as well as a couple of new plans to see. We talked about prices, time lines, and upgrades for a couple of hours. Then we agreed to meet in the morning when he would take me on a tour of the communities.

When I left his office, I drove to the greenbelt I'd passed this morning and parked the car. I sat there for a few minutes watching people running, riding bicycles, and some young women pushing strollers and chatting. These people were going to be my neighbors. I decided to take a little walk myself.

The spring air felt good and the blooms of flowers and trees brought a smile to my face. I thought of walking here with Jack Frost and him splashing in the Boise River to cool down in the summer. I'd walked about thirty minutes when I spotted an inviting bench and I sat down to watch some geese that were nesting near the water. Whatever the disruption of my spirit recently was, it seemed to be melting away. I could hardly wait to make this move. And knowing I didn't have to bring everything was actually a relief. All I had to do was pack what I could fit in the car along with Jack and Snowball. I took a deep, cleansing breath.

As I walked back to the car I remembered the question that had come in the night — *Could you give them up?*

That night back at the hotel, I couldn't stop thinking about the question I had heard. I got out my phone and opened my Bible app. *Maybe if I read a Psalm I can sleep — or at least find peace.* I felt I couldn't ignore the question any longer. *Lord, I don't know why you'd ask if I could give up Jack and Snowball. But if you are really asking me this — I have to tell you that I don't want to — and I don't understand why you're asking that of me. But I love you and trust you — and you'd have to find them a loving home.*

The next morning I woke early excited to meet with Cliff. We spent the morning together in his pickup truck, driving through the communities he'd already built houses in. He'd purposely designed the streets and houses for community. All the homes Cliff built had small front yards, and porches to bring neighbors together. Each community also had a family friendly park. He took me to an available lot on a street right across from the park, with houses on either side of it beautifully completed. Both homes had flowers and shrubs and lovely lawns that seemed to beckon a visitor to the porch.

We had gotten out of his truck so I could look around and take photos when a woman who appeared to be in her mid thirties came outside. A little boy followed right behind her.

"Hello, Cliff. What brings you here?"

He approached her and put out his hand. "Hi Robin. This is Amelia and she's interested in building a cottage. I think you ladies would make great neighbors."

Robin shook his hand then stepped toward me and extended her hand. "We love our home and neighborhood. The kids are all safe here; they can ride their bikes on the sidewalks, play in the park, and we have seasonal block parties! Do you have kids?"

I shook Robin's hand. "I do, but they're grown. I'm moving down here from Alaska and it's a big move so I want to be part of a close-knit community here." I looked down at the little boy. "What's your name?"

"I'm Austin and I'm four." He held up four fingers. "And I can read."

"Austin, it's nice to meet you and you must be a very smart boy! I like to read too. If I move here maybe we can read together sometime, if it's okay with your Mom."

His eyes crinkled as he smiled. "You want me to go get a book?"

"I'm afraid I can't right now, honey. Cliff is showing me around this morning."

Robin smiled and said, "Well if you move here I think you already have a friend." She laughed and ruffled her little boy's hair.

I couldn't help but smile. Having kids around to bake cookies for again would be nice.

Cliff said, "Thank you for coming out to say hi."

"Nice to meet you Amelia. Hope to see you soon! I think you'd be happy in our community."

Austin waved, "See you soon, Meely-ah."

Back at Cliff's office, I thanked him for spending so much time showing me around. We agreed I would stay in touch, and as soon as my house sold we could move forward. In the meantime, I could be making my decision on which lot and house plan I wanted to purchase. Ironically, I couldn't wait to get back home to Alaska, so that I could prepare for my move to Idaho!

The next day I had another HR tour scheduled that took up almost the entire morning. It wasn't that the facility was larger than the previous one, but the HR person giving me the tour seemed scattered, and it didn't help that she kept interrupting our tour to answer her phone. From what I overheard, the calls sounded more personal than business. In all fairness, I thought she might be going through a personal crisis. On a professional level I believed she should have taken the day off or had someone else show me around. That and the chaos I observed in another department led me to think that it wasn't clear who the manager was. I already knew I preferred the first hospital I'd toured this one might be fine for some, but for someone who had a great appreciation for order, it wasn't the one for me.

Since I had cancelled my plans to drive to Wyoming on this trip, I'd have four days to explore with no rigid schedule set in stone. I went to the lobby and picked up some brochures to take back to my room. I glanced at a couple before I decided I rather be seeing things in person. I pulled out the map of the city and surrounding areas, stuck a couple bottles of water in my bag, and headed out. I'd been online last night researching the area and had a list of places I wanted to go explore. I wanted to go by the University, and it's outlying areas. There were places to hike and parks to see, but I'd have plenty of time to do that after I moved, and having Jack with me would be more fun. It would be summer time when we moved, and the perfect season for us to explore and find our way around. I could hardly wait.

I returned to my hotel and decided to check my email. There was a message from Out of Africa.

I hope you are well. I would love to speak to you in person, but I respect your space. I have so enjoyed our communication. It makes my day to see messages from you. If you would like to talk — I'll be around for a week. I'm putting my phone number at the end of my message in case you would want to call. Take care.

At that moment, my phone rang. My heart sped up and my hand shook. I could hardly swipe the screen to answer. "Hello?"

"Yes, hi Amelia, it's Cliff. I'm hope I'm not disturbing you, but I wondered if you'd like to go to dinner? Uh, we could work on the cottage plan a bit. Just so I know exactly what you want while you're still here to clarify things."

It took me a second to realize that Out of Africa didn't have my phone number. Why did I think it would be his voice on the other end of the line, did I want him to call?

"Amelia? Are you there?"

"Yes, I'm here. I was momentarily distracted, sorry." I was a bit taken off guard when he mentioned having dinner, but since it was to go over plans, it might be a good idea. "Yes, I think that would work. My schedule is open. What time are you thinking?"

"Is five thirty okay? I should be able to get out of office and have time to clean up by then."

"Sure. Where should I meet you? I'll put the address in my map app on my phone."

"I thought I'd just pick you up at your hotel, if that works. No sense in taking two cars, or in you having to find your way around. And then I'll know you got back to your hotel safely too."

"I feel pretty safe here, but that's fine. Okay, I'll be watching for you. Thank you."

CHAPTER 13

*C*liff pulled into the pick up/drop off area at the hotel entrance. He got out of his truck and came around to open the door for me. I thought that was interesting because I'd been opening my door while we were out looking at his communities. As we drove to the restaurant, I couldn't help but notice that he was wearing cologne. Not too strong, spicy, pleasant. I hadn't worn fragrances in years because as a nurse that just wasn't acceptable — so many people had allergies. And being so used to not wearing it at work, in time I'd stopped wearing it altogether.

At dinner we chatted about Boise, then he pulled out some plans and spread them on the table. I was delighted at his ideas and made only a couple of changes that would fit my needs. After making notes, he rolled the plans and we talked a while. He shared that he'd grown up on a ranch in Idaho and an uncle had introduced him to building. He loved it but found his passion in developing communities. "I guess I was a Norman Rockwell fan as a kid." He laughed.

"Me too. The world has enough ugly in it — you see it plenty working in the hospital — I'm sure much more so in larger cities. But why not make it a better place as much as you can? I have to tell you, I checked into a few contractors and their ratings and chose you for two things — reviews on the quality of your work and for your community concept. Especially moving where I don't know anyone — having instant community is a huge plus."

"I'm glad you chose me. I feel honored and a bit flattered." He looked down and played with his coffee cup. "I'm looking forward to working with you. And I think it will be nice having you live here."

Suddenly I wanted to go back to my hotel. Cliff was polite, congenial and smelled nice, and I was curious to know more about him, but I felt hesitant about asking anything remotely personal. This was a professional relationship and I didn't want to start a new life and have someone mistakenly think I was interested in dating. It's best to have clear boundaries. Even at home where I had established clear boundaries, people still seemed determined to blur them — or maybe they just didn't understand them.

"That's kind of you to say." I smiled at him, but I felt tense. "Well, Maybe we should get our checks. It's been a long but productive day and I appreciate all your time. I guess that's why you have such great ratings."

"I invited you to dinner. I'll get the check. And it's a business meeting, so I can even write it off." He grinned.

I laughed. "Good thinking! Thank you for dinner."

We arrived at my hotel just before nine thirty. He again got out and came around to open my door, then walked me into the hotel. There were a number of men congregated in the bar area with drinks and a couple of them seemed to watch me. Cliff took my arm, leaned over and said, "Where is the elevator?"

I nodded towards the right and he walked me down the hall to the elevator. I felt a little weird — he'd been a perfect gentleman, but walking me to the elevator was over the top. "You are a kind gentleman, Cliff."

"I just wanted to make sure you got here safe."

The elevator door opened and I walked in. "Good night, and thank you." I went to my room and bolted the door. I smiled and sighed. It felt good to think someone had your back. Immediately I thought of Out of Africa's message. I opened up my laptop and read it again, then reached for a pen and the pad of paper on the desk and wrote down his number.

The rapid heart beat returned and my throat felt dry. I went to the refrigerator and pulled out a bottle of water and took a long drink. As though my throat had a hole in it, the water didn't help.

What am I thinking? I can't call him. But I picked up my phone. *What would I say? Lord, why do I feel like this? He seems like a Godly man and he's not even in Idaho. I'm not afraid — of him.* Suddenly, it was as if I'd walked into a commercial lighting store — the brightness of realization. *This isn't about this man — I'm afraid of myself. Of making bad decisions. Even though I've allowed you to heal my heart since Jeff died, I have held on to my plans and life with a tight fist. Please forgive me, Father for not trusting you in all things.*

I thought again of Jesus' disciples on the boat in the rough waters. I'm no different from them.

You can trust me. Give it all to me. You gave up the belongings but what I truly desire is to have all of you.

I set my phone down, dropped to my knees on the floor, and bowed my head. *Lord, I give it all to you. I don't want to be half in — I want to be submerged in You. I surrender all of me.*

Peace permeated my spirit. A joy filled me to running over. I got up and danced around the room. I laughed and realized others might be trying to sleep so I covered my mouth with a pillow and laughed into it while I danced.

After turning on the shower to heat up, I picked up my phone. I still felt at peace. I decided it was too late to call anyone, so I texted to the number I'd written down.

Hello Out of Africa. I hope this doesn't wake you. I know it's late but I just wanted to let you know we can talk.

I took a quick shower and got into my nightgown and crawled into the bed. I looked at my phone and there was a text message.

Dear one, I'm awake. Please call. I don't think I can sleep knowing you are only a phone call away. I don't want to call you in case you're trying to sleep.

I sat there for a minute looking at the message. Then I placed the call.

"Hello?" I could hear the smile in his voice.

"Hello. My name is Amelia. Crystal was a name I used for Strike a Match to retain anonymity."

"Dear Amelia — my name is Pete."

"Pete?" A rush of confusion filled my head.

"Yes, we've met before."

I sat back against the pillows, stunned. I couldn't find the questions I wanted to ask so we stayed there — hanging in the space of silence while I tried to figure out what was happening.

Finally I spoke. "Pete." Being an ER nurse, I'm pretty good at handling stressful or unpredictable situations — at work — but this was personal and I was at a loss.

"Amelia, first let me tell you I couldn't believe it when I saw your picture on Strike a Match. After meeting you in Las Vegas I kept hoping you would email me sometime. Since the day we first met, I have prayed for you every day. And then I ran into you at the hospital in Seattle. I was over the top thrilled to see you and again hoped you'd email me. I put it in God's hands."

I nodded, but knew he couldn't see me.

"One day I saw an ad for a free trial on Strike a Match. I'm not internet savvy but out of curiosity I signed up for the trial period and your profile came up. I couldn't believe it. My only explanation is that it had to be a God thing! I wondered why you signed up on there, but I know God allowed me to find you. Without a doubt. Even if it's only to be friends and now we can lift each other in prayer — it was worth it to find you."

I listened intently. A God thing? The timing of this — the fact that it happened at all was wilder than fiction. "I don't know what to say. I would have written to you after I saw you in Seattle."

"*Would* have? Why *didn't* you?"

I cleared my throat. "I didn't have your email address. To be honest, the day we met I was waiting for my next flight and I thought why would I want to write a guy in Vegas? So I threw your email address away. When you asked me to write when I saw you in Seattle — I don't know. I was so surprised — and then I was too embarrassed to tell you I'd thrown it away. My friend told me I'd know that seeing you that day wasn't a coincidence if I ran into you a third time. Why didn't you tell me who you were? And what are you doing in Montana?"

"*You* were using a pseudonym too. And I'm not in Montana any more than you are. I didn't want to scare you. I wanted to build a rapport and see what happened. And we became friends. Right?"

"Yes, we did. This is unreal."

"I'd really like to meet in person — for a third time. Is that possible?"

"I would like to see you again, Pete. I can't get more leave time though and I'm only here four more days."

"How about I drive down? Boise is only a little over an eight hour drive from Seattle. I can be there in time to take you to dinner tomorrow. What do you say? Will you have dinner with me?"

"I'd be happy to have dinner with you." I gave him the name and address of the hotel where I was staying.

"I'll send a text just before I get on the road."

"Good, then I'll have an idea of what time you might arrive so I wont' be worried. "He laughed. "You're sweet. I travel around the world and am not used to having someone concerned."

"I know that's not true. You have friends that care for you."

"Yes, I do have friends. Now I have a very special one. But you're not to worry. Trust."

"I know. God's working on that in my life. Good night, Pete."

"Good night, sweet pearl."

It was early morning before I could fall asleep. My mind wouldn't shut down. What were the chances of us connecting like this? On a plane in Nevada, in a hospital in Washington and then on the internet. And now our third face-to-face meeting will be in Idaho. Yes, it had to be a God thing.

After a whole three hours of sleep, I was afraid to look in the mirror. It was too early to go anywhere and too early to call Angie. I got dressed for the day, went to the dining room downstairs and had some orange juice, fruit, and bacon. I scanned a newspaper to get an idea of what might be available to rent when I moved, until my house was finished. It was way too early to consider temporary housing or buying a few pieces of furniture, but reading the rental advertisements gave me an idea of costs which would help in my budgeting.

I went up to my room to write a long email to Ang. Thirty minutes later my phone rang.

"Oh my word, Amelia! This is so amazing. I can't believe it. Are you serious?"

I laughed. "Hi, Ang. I know, it's crazy isn't it? What are the chances?"

"Chances? Do you honestly think this has anything to do with chances? Give me a break!"

"I honestly don't know what to think. But I could hardly sleep last night. And what's really wild is I had an awesome encounter with God last night before all this came about. I was thinking again on the sermon we heard when I visited you, and our discussion about the ship in the storm. Oh Ang, I realized that even though I allowed God to heal my heart from the past, I hadn't opened it to completely trusting Him for today — I've held on to control with a fist. And how silly is that? We can't control things. How about when I broke my ankle? What control did I have?"

"Wow, Mel. You inspire me. You're amazing."

"No, I'm not — not even close. But God is. Anyway, Pete will be here this evening and we're going to dinner.

"So where do you picture this going?"

"I think we will be long time friends. I think he's a special person."

"Well, he has to be, because you are. I know you'll be tied up, but text me when you can, okay?"

"Yes, mom. You know I always check in with you."

"Yep, I've got your back. I love you."

"I love you too. Pray for me, okay?"

"You got that."

I decided to explore a little this morning to occupy myself. I drove to an area I had read about and the first thing I noticed was a cute coffee shop — jackpot! The day is already off to a perfect start! After fueling up, I decided to stroll down the street that was lined with historic buildings. I strolled through art shops, couldn't resist a candy shop, and admired little bungalow type homes — some with wonderfully scented flowers along the sidewalk. Actually I was just killing time until Pete arrived. I have no use for art or fancy clothes, I'm a scrubs woman. I laughed to myself. And who knows, maybe I'll take up painting again someday — or not.

My phone chimed, notifying me that I had received a text message. I pulled it from my purse and saw that the message was from Pete. My heart seemed to beat a little faster.

I expect to arrive in Boise between five or six this evening. Can't wait to see you.

I texted back, *I'm looking forward to seeing you too. Drive safe.*

I said a prayer for his safety on his journey.

By early afternoon, my stomach growled, but if I ate something, I wouldn't want dinner. I went back to my car and drove for a while, familiarizing myself with the landscape. Although Idaho has mountains, Boise is rather flat, but it had several parks where walking or biking were popular and I loved the idea that there were plenty of places to meet people.

After a time I realized that I was anxious, so I parked the car near a park in town, and took a stroll by a lake. There were a couple of paddle boats occupied by happy people who waved as they passed by me. I smiled and waved back and thought it would be fun to bring Angie here. I spotted a rose garden and wandered through, stopping to breathe in the scent of the beautiful blooms. Idaho wasn't Alaska, but she had her own beauty and I was certain this was going to be a good transition. I appreciated that there was a longer season to enjoy the outdoors and I also enjoyed all the blooms.

I checked the time on my phone. Almost three in the

afternoon. I headed back to my hotel. I hit my forehead with the palm of my hand. I should have asked Pete if he wanted me to reserve a room for him. Well, he'd be here early enough to get a room I supposed.

After I freshened up, I put on a blue dress I'd brought. I was just putting on earrings when my phone rang.

"I'm in front of your hotel. Are we still on?"

I grabbed my room key and purse and dashed out the door and hit the elevator button three times. It probably took five seconds for it to open and I was ready to dash downstairs when it did. As it went down, I tried to take a deep breath. *Why do I feel like a teenaged girl?*

I practically ran through the lobby and out through the doors. I glanced around the parking lot and to the side I noticed an older dark green Subaru. Then I noticed the man with a baseball cap, fireman's mustache and a dark tan leaning against it. My heart raced, but I stopped in my tracks. We stood maybe twenty feet apart, neither of us moved. I wasn't sure if I should go to his car or let him come to me. Then I realized the man had just driven over eight hours to come to me — it was my turn to walk a few yards to go to him.

Nervous, I smiled and looked both ways to make sure a car wasn't coming. I felt as though I was floating rather than walking towards him. The closer I got, the bigger his smile. I stopped an arms distance away and we just stood there and looked at each other, eyes locked. I think we were both processing this — our third face to face encounter.

Finally I spoke. "Hi Pete." I opened my arms and he closed the gap and embraced me. I soaked in the strength of his arms around me, the scent of his soap, the comfort of my head on his shoulder. It was as though I had found solace. I held onto him and felt his face in my hair. My eyes began to burn and I closed them tightly. I didn't want runny mascara to ruin this moment — or his shirt. I couldn't stop the giggle that boiled up from inside. Still holding me by the shoulders, he leaned back to look at my face.

"Dear Amelia, are you crying?"

I had my hand over my mouth and giggled even harder. Now I was going to have a mascara problem for certain. But at least I wouldn't smear his shirt.

"What? Are you crying or laughing?" He looked concerned.

My giggle turned into laughter and I couldn't speak. I kept covering my face trying to gain control. The poor man would regret his long drive to see me.

He reached into his back pocket and pulled out a handkerchief and placed it in my hand. Thankfully it was blue so hopefully I wouldn't make such a mess of it. I wiped my eyes with my fingers.

He still had his hand on my left shoulder. "I'm starting to get a little scared. Does this mean that you're happy to see me?"

I nodded, but still couldn't speak. Waves of laughter hit me and the poor man stood there with his hand on my shoulder. The worst part came when I snorted. In my embarrassment I laughed harder which caused me to snort again — several times. Tears came down my cheeks like miniature waterfalls.

He put his arms around me and held me close. My laughter finally stopped but the tears didn't. I sensed people walking by — after all we were outside the main entrance of the hotel.

Finally my nerves calmed, but I was afraid to look up because I knew my mascara was running. Pete placed his hands on my shoulders and held me away from him to look at my face, but I put my head down. He put his finger under my chin and said, "Look at me."

Reluctantly I lifted my head. I was afraid to speak in case I started laughing or crying again. I was hysterical. And terribly embarrassed.

He looked into my eyes. "You're beautiful."

I tried to look down but he kept his finger under my chin.

"No, you look at me. You're beautiful. And you're kind of a mess." He grinned. "Let's go inside and you can wash your face before I take you out in public." He winked.

The giggles started to return but I was able to control them with deep breaths — barely.

In my room I looked on the mirrored tray that held shampoo, conditioner, lotion and found a make up remover cloth. I opened it and cleaned my face. Since the crazy emotions had come out of nowhere, I elected not to reapply any mascara.

When I arrived in the lobby, Pete was leaning against a column waiting for me. He smiled when I approached and opened his arms.

"Dear Amelia, let's try this again?"

I felt a giggle start in my gut, but took a deep breath and forced it down. I put my head up and walked into his arms. "Yes, let's."

When we approached his car, he opened the passenger door for me, handed me a bouquet of flowers, then went around the car to get in. "I made reservations for us. I hope you like Italian?"

"I do."

We were seated and our order taken. Pete ordered a spinach dip and Italian bread appetizer and leaned over to give me a bite. It felt so intimate. I fought a giggle again, but couldn't help smiling.

"What are you smiling about?"

"Our first date and already you have me eating out of your hand. What hope is there for me?" I knew I would have sore cheeks by the end of the evening from all the smiling, but I couldn't stop. This was the happiest I'd felt in — I didn't know when.

"Oh, I had that all planned — to have you eating out of my hand as soon as possible."

We chatted and laughed while we ate our meal and then we shared a dessert. When we got up to leave, every table and booth was occupied. I wondered where all those people had come from. I hadn't noticed a soul. Pete wrapped my sweater around my shoulders and put his hand on the small of my back to walk me out. It seemed that everyone we walked by was smiling at us. When he helped me into the car a man was driving through the parking lot and honked his horn and gave Pete a thumbs up. Pete grinned and gave him one back.

"Why were all those people smiling at us when we left? And where did they all come from?"

"They were smiling at you. They were there all along."

"Oh my, that's really strange. I felt as though we were all alone."

"That's why they were smiling. I think they saw two people deeply in love with each other."

I rode silently. Two people in love? People thought we were in love?

Pete interrupted my thoughts. "Amelia, do you have more business in Boise?"

"No, I've accomplished what I came to do. My time is free."

"I have a proposition."

"A what?"

"I have dear friends who live about ten hours from here. Unlike some people, they actually live in Montana."

He smiled. "They're prayer partners and I often stay with them a few days when I return from Africa to rest. I would so much like for you to meet them and show you around their ranch. What do you think?"

It sounds lovely, but I'm flying out from Boise. That'd be a lot of driving back and forth.

"Could you change your ticket? You could fly out of Billings? I'll pay for the change if you can."

I thought about it for a minute. Traveling by car can give one a lot of insight about the people they are traveling with. And being out of the city on a ranch sounded like fun.

"Sure, I'll call the airline right now."

After just a few minutes I had my reservation changed. "We're on. When do you want to go?"

He looked at the clock on the dashboard. "It's only eight thirty now. If I have you back to your hotel by nine, we could get an early start in the morning?"

"Okay. Oh, did you book a room while you were there? I should have thought to book one for you while you were driving down."

"I booked a room at a little place a couple miles away. I want to guard your honor."

"Well, of course, but you could have booked a room at the hotel where I'm staying."

"I thought it best to stay somewhere else." He looked at me and smiled. I know you're an early morning person because of when you have messaged me on Strike a Match. So are you up for getting an early start in the morning?

"What time are you thinking?"

"Can I pick you up at five or five thirty? Then we could be up there for the evening. Is that too early?

"Not at all, I'll be waiting at the door by five."

As soon as I got to my room, I dialed Angie and started packing. She was nearly laughing in hysterics herself, when I shared about meeting Pete.

"I'm not sure I'll be able to sleep," I said.

"I'll pray for you, Mel. This is so exciting. I wish I was a fly on the wall."

"No, you don't. I'd smash you. Flies are spawns of the devil."

She laughed. "True. Sweet dreams — that is if you get to sleep."

CHAPTER 14

We'd been on the road for a couple of hours when we drove through a little town and Pete asked if I was hungry.

"I suppose I could handle a bite to eat if you're getting hungry too."

Okay, I see two cafes. Which one is your desire?"

I pointed to one and Pete pulled into the parking lot. "If it's bad, it's your fault." He grinned.

"Oh so that's why you had me choose. Blame it on the woman." I smiled at him. "Okay, I have big shoulders. I can carry the blame."

"I'm teasing. God made my shoulders bigger so I could carry the responsibility."

I put my hands up. "All right I'll let you carry it."

He came around to open my door and we went inside. A few people were eating and a cook came from the back.

"How are you folks today?"

Pete said, "I don't know about her, but I'm blessed."

"Good to hear. I'm Donnie and this is my place. Do you know what you want to eat?"

I said, "Good morning, Donnie. Could we have a minute to look at your menu? We're actually not from here."

"Oh sure. And if you want something that's not listed, ask — maybe I can make it for you."

A young woman brought us both water and Pete a cup of coffee, then she took our order. We didn't wait long for our food to arrive. Donnie brought it himself. He looked at Pete.

"Why are you blessed?"

"Because I'm in the company of this beautiful, young woman."

Donnie looked over at me and nodded.

"And because I know Jesus as my Savior. I was lost in my sin and selfishness and He gave me new life and new purpose."

"I wish I knew Jesus like that. My wife has cancer and my daughter suffers with health issues. I'm trying to hold my family together and run this place too."

My heart went out to Donnie. "Donnie, can we pray with you right now?"

He nodded and I reached for his hand and then for Pete's hand. The three of us bowed our heads and we prayed for Donnie, his family and his business. When we finished Donnie had tears in his eyes. "I think God must have sent you here today. I've gotten so wrapped up in my problems — I stopped giving them to Him some time ago. Thank you."

We continued on our journey and Pete glanced over at me, smiled, reached out for my hand and held it as he drove. A peace seemed to envelope us. Being with Pete felt so natural and easy. Almost as if we'd always been together.

A little more than four hours later, Pete pulled over. "There's hot springs here. Would you like to get out and have some lunch?"

"Is there a place to eat nearby?"

Pete turned and reached into the back seat and pulled out a cooler. "Depends. How hungry are you?"

"Seriously? You packed a picnic? Were you a boy scout?"

He laughed. Nope, but I'm a paramedic and I like to be prepared. So, are you hungry?"

He opened my door for me then grabbed the cooler and set it on a picnic table. He pulled out deli sandwiches, fruit, veggies, chips and drinks. "Oh, I have paper towels in the car." He went to grab them and I opened the fruit and veggies. He came back with the roll of towels and tore one off for each of us. "I tried to get a variety. You can have half of each sandwich or pick one." We sat down and he took my hand and bowed his head, gave thanks for the food, travel safety, and me. After our picnic I went to put my toe in the hot springs.

"Wait! It's hot." He grabbed my arm.

I stuck my toe in anyway then jerked it back. "Ow! It's hot." I looked over at him and we both laughed.

He looked up. "The woman has to learn to trust me, Lord." He looked over at me and winked.

We arrived at the ranch about six that evening. His friend came out to greet us. They grabbed hands and bantered back and forth a bit and then Pete introduced us. Royce led the way into the house. "Livia's in the kitchen throwing food."

"Is everything okay?" I wondered if we'd come at a bad time.

"Oh, I reckon so — she just said she was going to toss a salad." His laugh was big and full.

Livia looked up from her task as we entered. "I'd shake your hand Pete, but I'm holding a knife."

"I'll wait. Don't want to get stabbed in the back. Been there, done that." He made a face.

"That's how you learned not to hug women holding knives, huh?" Livia laughed.

Pete introduced us, and I instantly knew I loved these new friends.

"Can I help with anything, Livia?"

"You can grab the dressing out of the fridge and put butter on the table for the rolls."

I liked that she allowed me to jump in. I felt at home.

Pete went outside with Royce while Livia and I got out dishes and silverware. In just a few short minutes the guys came back in with a plate of huge steaks. I was still working on my steak when Livia set a large berry pie on the table. Royce and Pete dug into it. It looked so good I wanted to try it, but I was so full. I looked at Pete's pie and he cut a bite with his fork and lifted it to me.

I held up my hand. "No, that's too much, you eat it."

He laughed and cut a smaller bite and lifted it to me. I happily ate it, relishing the bright berry taste in my mouth.

A couple hours after dinner, Pete and I headed into the small town twenty minutes away. When we pulled in the parking lot of a hotel he said, "Here's where you're going to stay."

"Are you sure? It looks closed."

"It doesn't open for tourists for another couple of weeks but I called ahead and asked if they could ready one room for a lady coming to town. I thought you'd be more comfortable — and feel safer — in your own room. Royce and Livia came by to check on it earlier."

He went to the office door and knocked. A moment later a man opened the door and handed him a key. Pete came back to the car, grabbed a little cooler and a bag along with my carry-on. "Let me go make sure it's got everything you need and I'll come back for you."

My room was right next to the office on the first floor. When I entered the room, I thought we were in the wrong place.

There were flowers on the table, and a basket that held Peppermint Patties and packages of microwave popcorn. Pete pointed and said, "There's water in the fridge."

I opened the fridge to find Honeycrisp apples, dates, natural peanut butter, little cups of yogurt and bottles of water. All things I had mentioned at one time or another. Some on the plane during our first meeting. "How did you do this? Have you been taking notes since we met?"

He smiled. "Do you like it? I'm a planner. I was up early this morning and enlisted a little help from some friends." He pointed at the flowers.

"Wow. I'm overwhelmed."

"You get some rest. If you need anything the number for the office is by the bed and you have my number. Can I pick you up for breakfast?"

I waved my hand around me toward the fridge. "I thought all this was breakfast."

He walked to the door and stopped. "Are you okay?"

"I'm great. Thank you. You're a thoughtful man." I took the two steps to accept his open arms. We shared a warm hug before he pulled away.

"Good night, pearl. Lock the door as soon as I go out."

The next morning he texted me and asked if I was ready for the day. I called him. "I'm up, already read my Bible, and am about to hop in the shower. Can you give me thirty minutes?"

We ate at a little cafe a couple of blocks from the hotel. Everyone seemed to know each other. After we ate, he drove us toward the mountains. "Ready for a little hike?"

"I am." I grabbed a couple of waters while he strapped a gun to his hip for protection due to mountain lion sightings.

We walked through some thickets and brush. He took my hand and as we walked he pointed out signs of elk, as well as trails and markings that revealed various animals traveled this way frequently. We approached a big rock and stopped.

"I wanted to bring you here. This is a special place to me. I call it *Prayer Rock* and I come here often when I'm at the ranch. It's peaceful, and I can be all alone and pour out my heart to God. I wanted to share it with you. Will you climb up with me?"

I nodded and he gave me his hand to assist my climb. My tennis shoes weren't quite as good as climbing boots would have been, but with his help I made it to the top without any issues.

He prayed first. He thanked God for third chances, for me, and this time together. And asked for God's will. When it was my turn, I thanked God for this time together and all the things He was doing in my life, and the new adventures ahead. We sat quietly on the rock, holding hands and basking in the presence of God.

When we finally climbed down from the rock, Pete said, "Have you ever shot a nine millimeter?"

I shook my head. "I don't even know what it is."

He pulled the gun from the holster and removed the ammo from his pocket. "We just as well make use of the trash the inconsiderate people have left behind." He lined up some beer cans, a milk jug and a few bean cans. He explained how the gun worked and the safety precautions. I'd shot a twenty two when I was a kid, but that was a long time ago. To make sure I was comfortable with the firearm. He stood behind me and guided me through the process of shooting at the first milk jug. Once I signaled that I was comfortable, he stepped to the side. I took aim at the lined up targets and popped each one.

"Whoa. Maybe I'll just hang onto the gun." He laughed as he checked to make sure no bullets were in the chamber before he placed the gun back in the holster. He collected the targets in a plastic bag and carried the bag in one hand while holding my hand with the other.

Next he drove us to a beautiful, crystal lake in the mountains. We climbed a little bit then sat and watched fish bubble. When I shivered from the mountain breeze on my bare arms, he wrapped his arm around me and I found myself leaning into him as though it was something I'd always done. I surprised myself. I felt so open with him.

"Maybe we should go back to town and get something to eat?"

"There's plenty of food at the hotel, we don't need to buy food."

"But that's for you."

"You don't honestly think I can eat all that? We'll share."

"Will that be enough until dinner? I want to take you out to dinner."

"Pete, it's plenty. And I budgeted for my trip to Idaho. You don't need to buy me meals. That gets expensive. Let me treat you to dinner. You drove all the way from Seattle, packed a picnic, drove all the way up here. You have taken care of me like ..."

"Like a pearl of great value. And you are. Amelia, I love you."

He stood up and reached for my hand. I stood up and looked into his eyes — and then I kissed him. A little test-the-waters kiss. He couldn't hide his surprise. Before he could react I leaned up to kiss him again, but he leaned down to meet my lips. The lake and trees, the mountains and sky — all swirled around us — or maybe my head was spinning.

He seemed to try to catch his breath. "I hoped for that at some point, but I sure didn't see it coming." We stood there looking into each other's eyes, searching. I think he wanted to hear me declare my love. But I couldn't do that. I had to be positive it was true. I felt it was true, but I didn't want to say it lightly. And the last time I'd declared my love — it'd turned out to be a disaster. I was a little scared.

That afternoon he dropped me off at the hotel and he went back to the ranch to shower. When he came back, he said, "I made you dinner."

"Seriously? You cook too?"

He smiled and went back out. A few minutes later he returned to get me. He led me to the hotel office where a small round table was set with a candle, table cloth, and cloth napkins in rings. He opened a cooler and pulled out containers. He pulled out a chair for me at the table, poured me a small glass of wine and served me seasoned rice, African peanut sauce over chicken, green beans and crusty bread. The aroma of the meal made my stomach growl.

He was such a thoughtful person. "Pete, this is wonderful. You're a multi talented man. You amaze me."

He chuckled. "Well, I'm not as talented as you think. My mind was on you the whole time I prepared the meal, and I had the sauce completely done when I realized I'd forgotten to put the chicken in. I had to thaw it and cook it. I'm not sure Livia and Royce will let me live that down." He laughed. "Now you know I'm not perfect."

I smiled. "I've been cooking for years and I still have my failures in the kitchen. But this is not a failure — it's delicious."

After lingering over the meal while we talked, I helped him pack everything. He put it back in his car then we went back to the hotel room. There was one little straight back chair in the room so we sat on the bed talking. I piled the pillows at the head so we could lean back on them. We held hands and chatted for a while before he leaned in to kiss me. I eagerly received his kiss. Another kiss followed. He wrapped his arms around me and leaned me back and I melted into his arms.

My heart raced — our breathing increased — I felt warm, tingly, heady. And then he was gone, bringing me back to reality. I looked over the edge of the bed to see him lying on the floor.

"Are you okay?"

He nodded.

"What are you doing on the floor?"

"God said, *'You need to stop this — now.'* So I threw myself off the bed."

"Were you afraid it was getting out of hand?"

"My thoughts were getting out of hand."

I stood up and reached down for his hand. He took it and stood up. "I'm sorry, Amelia."

"Me too. Pete? Thank you."

He leaned down and kissed my forehead. "Good night, Amelia. Lock the door. I'll call you in the morning?"

"I'll be waiting."

Lying in bed later, the evening ran over and over in my mind. He'd treated me with so much respect. And although I had no intention of doing anything sinful, I had to admit desire had been awakened. But he'd thrown himself on the floor for me. *Wow.*

The next morning we met up with Royce and Livia for breakfast. Conversation and laughter came easily. After breakfast we all went back to the ranch and rode four wheelers into the mountains. We stopped now and then to breathe in the view and take pictures. It felt so comfortable to ride behind Pete, my arms wrapped around his waist. When evening came, Livia suggested we grill hamburgers. Again she allowed me to work alongside her in the kitchen. Throughout the evening we all talked and laughed as though the four of us had known each other for years. Livia was like a sister. Easy to talk to, and laugh with. Someone I felt would be a friend for life.

Pete took me back to the hotel for the last time. He said we would head out early in the morning to make the two hour drive to Billings for my flight home. *Home.* I wondered where exactly was home now?

While we waited for my flight to board, Pete held my hand. I didn't want to leave. How absurd. I felt like I was leaving my heart behind. I kept my head on his shoulder so he wouldn't see my tears, but I kept sniffling. He pulled out a handkerchief and placed it in my hand.

My flight was called and he walked me as far as he could. We stopped and held hands, looking into each other's eyes. Mine kept spilling. "I love you," I whispered.

"What? Say it again."

That made me smile through my tears. "I love you. I don't want to leave you."

"Oh sweetheart, I've waited to hear you say those words. But you have to go now. We both have things we need to take care of. He pulled me into a tight hug. My tears spilled on his shirt.

As I walked out to the plane, I kept looking back and he was there — smiling, waving. And it looked like he was wiping his eyes.

I had a 2 hour wait in the Seattle Airport for my flight back to Alaska. I ate slices of apple while I sat at my gate watching people. I thought about my little cottage in the lovely community. I got up to toss my trash in the can and stopped. This was the very place I'd thrown away Pete's email address. Who could have imagined what had happened since that moment.

I called Ang, but she didn't answer. I left her a message. "Ang, it's me. We have to talk tomorrow. We have *so* much catching up to do!"

~

Jack Frost jumped in circles, barked, and wagged all around the room when I arrived home. I sat on the floor so he wouldn't knock me over in his exuberance. "I missed you too, boy." I scratched his ears and soon Snowball moseyed over to welcome me home in her, 'I don't want to over react' way.

Margie stood aside and laughed at the ebullient welcome home. "You are one little happy family. Maybe I need to get a dog. But I rent and I'm not sure I want the responsibility. But it's fun taking care of your animals. But then it might be because they're at your house, and I like being here. The view is spectacular and it's peaceful. And there's good food here. But I think I about finished it off so I just as well go home." She giggled.

"I'm glad there was enough to get you through the week. Thank you so much for taking care of everything. "Margie, I want to give you some money for watching the animals so often.

"Absolutely not. I should pay you for the privilege of staying in your house and eating your food. You could use a nice easy chair though." She laughed.

After she left I threw my clothes in the wash and made a grocery list and a list of things I needed to do in the next couple of days. I had to go to town the next day so I took a shower and went through the stack of mail that Margie had left on the kitchen counter. She'd left the house in good order so there wasn't much I had to do as far as that was concerned.

I decided to catch up with my email. There was a fair amount that I simply deleted, then I dealt with the rest. There was an email from Cliff with property information and a file that showed the tweaks I had made on the cottage plan that he and I had discussed. I closed my eyes and thought of how pleasant it was there. This move couldn't happen soon enough — I was ready. Well mentally, but I had a lot of things to do still. I decided it would be a good time to deal with the office files. There were only a few tax things I needed but I'd already saved them to a flash drive so they could be shredded.

As I ran the paper through the shredder, I missed my grandkids. They loved the job of shredding paper. They would have loved it today. There was so much paper that the shredder over heated and I had to let it cool down twice. That's when they would have taken a cookie break. But they are older and more independent now. Sports and plays and church activities. They are healthy, happy kids. We talked on the phone now and then, but with the family schedule, not as much as I would have liked.

One nice thing about Idaho was that it was a lot closer to Wyoming, so I could visit them and they could come see me. I knew it would be hard to get much time off from a new job, but it would be fun to have them come stay with me for a week or two when they were out of school.

There were so many things I could do with them, bike ride, rent a boat, hike, and of course bake cookies. I knew they'd never outgrow eating cookies — my sons hadn't. And now Tyson was living in the states too. I was excited that we'd all be in fairly close proximity again. I mean six hours was nothing compared to over two thousand miles or across the world.

I carried a box into work and set it down in the break room before I changed into scrubs and went to get a frozen drink. Nicole came in the break room.

"Mel, you're back!" She came over to hug me. "It seems like you've been gone for months."

I hugged her back. "I guess it has been months. Six weeks off with my ankle, here a couple of weeks, then gone again. Talk about a slacker." We laughed.

"So how did your trip go?"

"AMAZING."

"Really? You're going to have to tell me about it."

"I'm running down to get my frozen drink. Want one? I'm buying."

"Sure, I'll come with you."

"Do you know which doc is on today?"

"Martinez."

We got our drinks and I got a caramel macchiato for Dr. Martinez. He loves caramel or cinnamon anything.

As I approached his work station he said, "Welcome back stranger."

I handed him his drink.

He looked surprised. "What's this for?"

"For you. Enjoy."

Several people stood around the nurses station. I said, "Hey guys, I made lasagna and breadsticks last night for lunch today. They're in the break room so help yourself when you get hungry."

Josh came over and hugged me. "We missed you like crazy. No one else takes it on themselves to feed us around here."

"Josh, you know the docs buy lunch sometimes on busy days."

"Yeah, that's right. But those aren't made with love." He blew me a kiss.

Dealing with patients that day was like running a hot knife through butter. Smooth. It seemed nothing could upset me.

The next day I had just finished charting on a patient who had been discharged when Sheila came through.

188 | ELISA MARIA HEBERT

"Hi, how are things going today?"

I looked up. "Hi, Sheila. Good to see you."

"Yes, you've been gone a while. I'm glad you're here, I've been wanting to talk to you. Do you have a minute?"

"Absolutely. Just finished. What's up?"

"You know I bought a little house in town last fall."

"Yes, and it's adorable. How'd it do through the winter?"

"Snug as a bug. Now that I have my own place I've been thinking about getting a dog."

"That's a great idea. They are good company."

"I just love Jack Frost."

"He's a doll."

"This probably sounds funny, but if you ever had to give him up, would you consider me? Of course Snowball could come too because they are a pair!'"

I was about to take a drink of water but set it down. I felt — what did I feel? "Wow, Sheila. Thank you. If I ever had to give him up, I absolutely would consider you."

She touched my shoulder. "I need to make rounds. You look different Mel — happy."

"Aren't I usually happy?"

"Yes, you are. But now you have a glow."

I smiled. "Maybe."

"It looks great on you. You look so — great." Her pager buzzed and she pulled it from her pocket to look at it."Duty calls. See you later, Mel."

When she walked away I sat there feeling a little stunned. I remembered my prayer, 'You'd have to find them a loving home.' *God? What are you up to?*

CHAPTER 15

*T*uesday was my last shift for the week. Sophie and Grace had been working with me on inventory and we stopped for a break. Rather than go to the break room to take an official break, we sat at the nurses station. Katy came to return a patient to Ellen.

"Hey, Mel. You seem different. What's going on?"

"Different? How?"

Sophie said, "Yes she does."

Grace said, "It must be love. After all, it's spring somewhere in the world."

We all laughed. "So what is it, Mel?" Katy asked. She sat down.

"I met someone."

The three younger women all leaned in and I laughed.

"Where did you meet him? I thought you didn't date? Why wouldn't you let me give your number to my dad? And wait — what about Dr. Fletcher?"

"Was that a question or inquisition, Katy?"

"Sorry, but I do have a lot of questions." She leaned back and the other two nodded.

"Well it's a long story but maybe I do need to share some of it with you. I met this man while I was in Idaho. Actually I'd met him twice before — in passing. He drove to Idaho to meet for the third time. He wanted to drive me to Montana to meet some friends of his."

Katy said, "Oo la la. This is getting steamy now." She leaned closer.

"Yes, it got steamy. First off, he rented a hotel room for me away from where he was staying. He wanted me to feel safe. That in itself was proof that he valued and respected me.

Anyway, he took me back to my hotel the last evening and there was just one chair in my room, so we sat on the bed. We talked for a while before he kissed me and one kiss led to another. The situation heated up until we found ourselves horizontal — and then he threw himself on the floor."

"Wow," Sophie said.

"Why would he do that?" Katy asked.

I looked at Katy. "He said he wanted to treat me with respect, so he put a stop to things. He honored me by not trying to take advantage of the situation."

She sat there with her mouth partly open. "But why?"

"Katy, not all men are out to vandalize women."

"What do you mean, vandalize?"

"I mean to steal what isn't theirs and then run away. Your love is a gift that someone should treasure. But if you don't see the value in it, why would a guy? Giving yourself to someone is something to do inside of a loving, mutually respectful relationship. It shouldn't be given away like a lollipop in the bowl at the bank — just up for grabs."

"Well, I've never met a man who would throw himself on the floor for me. They just throw their clothes on the floor." She let out a weak laugh.

"Maybe you're meeting the wrong kind of men? And maybe the bar isn't the place to find the right kind of man? Maybe they think you don't really want love because you are available there? Katy, you deserve so much more."

"I'm not sure about that."

"I am. Living with a constant broken heart and looking for a new man all the time is not the plan God had for your life. You are precious. You are valued. You are loved by God. Don't sell yourself short."

Her eyes got watery. "I need to get back to work. I'm happy for you, Mel."

I had an hour before my shift was over. We had called the surgeon for a patient with a burst appendicitis and anesthesiologist came to see the patient before surgery. He found me replacing an oxygen tank. "Mel, it's good to see you. How are things?"

"Hi Rick, I haven't seen you in a while. I'm well, and you?"

"Fine. I was just thinking about you the other day. I haven't seen you since the barbecue at my brother's house."

"That's been a while."

"I heard that you and Mitch were seeing each other?"

I laughed. "Well, what you heard was a rumor."

"It sounded like it was serious. You took a trip together?"

"Oh brother, no, we flew out on the same flight going different places."

He looked around the room, towards the door, then back to me. "So does that mean you're still available?"

"Well, I don't know that I've ever been available."

"I just asked because if you aren't seeing him, but you're on the market, I'd like to take you to dinner. That is if you're interested."

I felt my face heat up. I never realized Rick had been interested in me. He used to stop and talk to me all the time in my old department, but that was years ago. "That is very sweet of you, Rick. The truth is, I'm in the middle of preparations to move out of Alaska."

"Oh. Guess I'm a day late and a dollar short." He laughed. "Well, I'd still like to take you out anytime, that is if you want. Even as a friend."

I wanted to express that I was flattered without encouraging him. "Rick, I appreciate the thought. I've always found you to be a congenial, pleasant man, but I wasn't interested in dating anyone. Thank you for your invitation though."

He left the ER and I watched him go. *That was a surprise.*

That evening as soon as I had cared for the critters and took a shower, I texted Pete to let him know I was home. My phone rang almost immediately.

"Sweet pearl, how was your day?"

"Fine. And yours?"

"I was distracted by thoughts of you."

"Shouldn't you be packing?"

"Oh, I'm packed already. I do that way ahead of time."

"When do you leave?"

"The day after tomorrow."

I felt a pang. "I'll miss talking to you."

"Not any more than I'll miss you."

"Pete, can I ask you a question?"

"Anything."

"What drives you to go to Africa?"

"I believe God told me to go. And I have skills and medicine to heal people."

"But why there?"

"Amelia, when I was in Viet Nam — I was responsible for a lot of death. For nearly twenty years I tried to drown those memories with whiskey. One night I was at the end of myself and was about to take my life. I spoke to God — angrily — that I didn't believe in Him.

Don't ask me how I could talk and be angry with

someone I didn't believe in — I didn't make a lot of sense in those days. He stopped me from taking my life that night. I found a Bible in the fire station and began reading and it came to life — as though He was speaking directly to me."

"It does speak to us, if we read with an open heart."

"I was able to pray over patients as I transported them to the hospital but it seemed there was more for me to do. Then ten years later the opportunity opened for me to go to Africa. I didn't want to go at first, but realized God was opening a door for me to do more. And I felt it was a way to redeem myself, even the least bit, for what I was ordered to do in Nam."

"I'm sorry for the way you were treated, Pete. I didn't understand what was going on."

"We didn't either."

We talked for over an hour. It seemed we had so much to say to each other and I felt I needed to say everything now, while I had the chance. He would be gone and I needed to move forward with my plans for Idaho. The only thing holding me back was the sale of my house.

I wish I'd kept track of how many people at work told me I seemed to glow with happiness. Even patients asked if I was in love. Was it really that obvious?

I hadn't heard from Pete because he worked in bush villages without access to phone service or internet. I hated that I found myself worrying about him. He'd spent years there and did just fine before he met me.

Five and a half weeks had passed with no word and I was still waiting on my house to sell so I could move forward and start the cottage in Idaho.

One warm, spring afternoon — Alaska was working her

magic — melting snow and ice. I took Jack Frost for a nice long walk. It felt so good to be outside and moving. As Jack and I descended a hill, my phone rang. "Hello?"

"Amelia — Robert Ide here."

"How are you Robert?"

"I'm well and I have some news for you."

"Does someone want to see the house? I thought it would be shown more."

"Not to worry. I'm very particular about showing homes. I want them to match the buyer so I don't show lots of houses to lots of people. I felt the couple I brought through the first time were the perfect match. Then they went back to the states because an elderly relative was ill which delayed their plans. I got a call an hour ago asking if your house was still on the market. They made a generous offer. I'd like to meet and go over it with you."

"Wow. That's great news! When do you want to meet?"

"How about in a couple of hours? Let's get this offer accepted."

"Okay, I'll see you at your office."

I clicked my phone off and stuck it in my pocket. "Jack, we have an offer on the house! We're going to be able to move soon." He wagged his tail and we turned to walk the thirty minutes back home. I found myself torn between being excited about the house and sad about missing Pete.

Why did love hurt? We had declared our love, but we were like two ships passing in the night. I supposed we'd always just be passing each other. I wasn't interested in dating anyone else. I knew I'd always love Pete, even if it was from a distance. On the up side of that, he'd have someone praying for him whenever he was gone. I knew he ministered medicine to villagers and Muslim prisoners. Unlike prisons in America, if family or friends didn't bring food or medicine, the prisoner would die.

About five minutes from home my phone rang again and I pulled it from my pocket. "Livia? How are you? Is everything okay?"

"Hi Amelia. Everything is great here. How about you?"

"I'm doing well. Just got an offer on my house."

"That's good news. I'm calling because Royce is sending a package up to you by air. Can you pick it up at the airport?"

"Sure. Just give me the specifics. Please tell Royce hello."

"Will do. I'll have him send you the information."

Royce texted me later with the specifics. Someone they knew was flying up on Friday at midnight and would deliver the package. I had to meet them at the airport. Easy enough.

It was well after midnight and I was in the terminal with many other people. Three flights were due in and two of those were late so all would be arriving at once. As I waited, I chatted with some soldiers and other people nearby. "Who are you waiting for?" I asked.

"We're here to welcome new soldiers in."

"Well, at least they have a nice sunny night to welcome them."

The sergeant laughed. "Yes, that will be a pleasant surprise to them. How about you? Waiting for family?"

"No, some friends sent a parcel up and I'm meeting the person who is delivering it for them."

We continued to chat and banter and eventually people began to arrive. We all watched and waited. I meant to ask Royce how their friend and I would recognize each other. Shoot. It was too late to call and ask him now because it was three in the morning in Montana. I saw military folks coming towards the baggage area, then I saw a lone man. He wore khaki pants, a white shirt and a safari hat. He stopped and knelt down before he reached the double doors that separated the arriving passengers from those who awaited them. He took off his hat and looked around. Then he stood up.

My heart skipped a beat. Maybe two, or three. Actually I thought it was coming up with a whole new rhythm. I saw the dark tan, the fireman mustache. He spotted me. He smiled and tilted his head in my direction before he came through the doors. I froze.

The sergeant glanced at me. "Is that who you're waiting for? He seems to know you."

I managed to nod my head and then slowly approached. "Pete."

He looked at me intently and I felt swallowed up in those glacier blue eyes. "Amelia." He dropped down on one knee and opened his hand to reveal a small, blue, velvet box.

"Precious pearl, will you marry me?"

I began to shake. I put my hand over my mouth and started to bend down. I put my other hand on his shoulder to steady myself. My eyes filled with tears and I nodded. I moved my hand from in front of my mouth. "What are you doing here? Really? Pete. Yes."

He smiled and removed my left hand from his shoulder and placed a ring on my finger. "That's the word I was waiting for. You said, *yes!*" He stood, grabbed me around the waist and swung me around. "She said yes!"

The crowd of people I'd been waiting with, clapped and called out congratulations. The Sergeant came over to shake Pete's hand, followed by a line of people who reached out to shake his hand or pat him on the shoulder and offer us their congratulations.

Tears streamed down my cheeks and I couldn't stop smiling. I remembered when I was a child and my mom would say, "Your face is going to freeze like that."

I hope so.

AFTERWORD

If you enjoyed this story, I would be grateful if you would take a moment to post a review on Amazon, and or Goodreads and tell your friends about it.

If you want to hear updates about Amelia and Pete's story, click this link to visit my page:
    www.ElisaMariaHebert.com
    You can spread the word by 'liking' my author page:
    https://www.facebook.com/ElisaMariaHebert

Watch for more of Amelia and Pete's story in the next book:
    No Elephants In Africa
    Coming in 2020.

ABOUT THE AUTHOR

Elisa Maria Hebert spent most of her life surrounded by the majestic beauty of Alaska. After meeting and marrying her sweetheart, she now finds herself surrounded by sunflowers in Kansas, along with their yellow lab and golden-doodle.

Elisa and her husband enjoy exploring and have even adventured as far as Africa to serve with a mission organization. At home they have plenty of excuse to travel, having children and grandchildren living in seven states from Alaska to South Carolina, and even Hawaii.

At home, Elisa enjoys cooking, flower gardening, quilting, entertaining, music and laughter.

facebook.com/ElisaMariaHebert@ElisaMariaHebert

goodreads.com/ElisaMariaHebert